ICE LORD'S BRIDE

Bride of the Fae, Book 1

Ava Ross

ICE LORD'S BRIDE

Bride of the Fae, Book 1

Copyright © 2022 Ava Ross

All rights reserved.

No part of this book may be reproduced in any form or by any electronic or mechanical means, including information storage and retrieval systems, without written permission from the author, except for the use of brief quotations with prior approval. Names, characters, events, and incidents are a product of the author's imagination. Any resemblance to an actual person, living or dead is entirely coincidental.

Cover by The Book Brander

Editing/Proofreading by Owl Eyes Proofs & Edits

AISN: B0B5M5S2K1

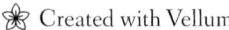 Created with Vellum

Foreword

A note to the reader.

If you found this book outside of Amazon,
it's likely a stolen/pirated copy.
Authors make nothing when books are pirated.
If authors are not paid for their work,
they can't afford to keep writing.

*For my mom who
always believed in me.*

Series by Ava

Mail-Order Brides of Crakair

Brides of Driegon

Fated Mates of the Ferlaern Warriors

Fated Mates of the Xilan Warriors

Holiday with a Cu'zod Warrior

Galaxy Games

*Alien Warrior Abandoned/
Shattered Galaxies*

Beastly Alien Boss

Bride of the Fae

Screamer Woods
Orc Me Baby One More Time

Stranded With an Alien
Frost

You can find my books on Amazon.

ICE LORD'S BRIDE

**I must marry one of the fae,
but the forbidden ice lord wants *me*.**

To secure a human-fae truce, I'm one of six women traveling to their magical kingdom, where we'll be courted by fae aristocracy. We have one month to choose a husband from among them.

Only Elion, the arrogant, beastly ice lord, is forbidden. His torturous scars make the other women gasp. His icy words rip them to shreds. His touch is colder than frost. He lurks in the shadows, never coming out into the light.

One stolen moment with Elion, and I'm intrigued. A kiss, and I'll do anything to call this brutishly handsome lord mine.

Then one of the women is found dead. When *you're*

next appears on my bedroom wall, written in blood, it's clear there's more going on here than solidifying the human-fae truce. If I'm not careful, I won't become a bride of the fae. I'll wind up dead.

Ice Lord's Bride is book one in a fantasy romance duology. It heats to a high sizzle and comes with a guaranteed happily ever after.

Warning: Don't read this book unless you're open to steamy romance, mystery & danger, and you're intrigued by the idea of becoming a bride to a scarred face ice lord.

Chapter 1
Raven

"Raven," my cousin, Jenny, hissed, her sneaker-clad feet dancing. She stood beside me while I waited for the next order to be thrust through the diner's kitchen window. We'd grown up like sisters and when I moved back to town, she'd gotten me this job. "Check out the dudes who just settled in booth three. I think they're *fae guys*." She breathed the last two words.

My gaze fell on the four men who'd slid into the corner booth of *Betty's Barnyard Biscuits*.

Yeah, there was no need to look twice. Definitely fae.

"What gave them away?" I teased. "Is it their height?"

"Seven feet of drool-worthy muscle," she sighed, sagging against me.

"Or maybe it's their long, glittering hair?" I added.

"I'm going to add sparkles to my own hair." She stroked her shoulder-length blonde tresses. "I picked up a kit at the pharmacy the other day. I'm adding glitter to mine this weekend. I'm doing Emme's too. She begged."

"Oh, she did, did she?" I wasn't surprised. My eight-year-old sister loved sparkles. She also loved Jenny. I'd bailed on this town six years ago, when I was eighteen to her two, and Jenny had stepped in to play big sister to Emme.

Ever since the fae revealed they existed among us; they were all we mortals could talk about. But after the initial splash and the news reports of the treaty they were negotiating with our government, we'd subsisted mostly on rumors. The press splashed pictures of the gorgeous diplomats, and man, I could see why Jenny gushed. Let's just say that these guys were featured in *many* of my late-night fantasies.

After lowering the full tray she was carrying onto the end of the bar, Jenny fussed with my brown hair I'd secured in a messy knot on the top of my head this morning before rushing from my apartment. "How about you? Should we give you sparkles too?"

"Nope." My one true claim to fame was my thick chestnut hair with natural gold highlights. At least I had one point in my favor. I hated my too-big nose— "It's distinctive, dear!" my grannie always used to say; and the tiny dimple in my chin—angel kissed, my grannie would then add, tapping the dent. I hated how short I was at five-two. My average build didn't make me stand out in a crowd. Okay, I could stand to lose a few pounds, but I loved whoopie pies. Who doesn't?

"Do you think they're part of the group signing the treaty?" Jenny asked, peering at the guys over her shoulder. Fortunately, they appeared to be too interested in their menus to notice her stare.

"You think the king of the fae would lower himself to eat at *Betty's Barnyard Biscuits*?"

"Why not? The food's good."

I lifted her gaping jaw. "I imagine they're part of the regular old diplomatic group." While we were quite a distance from Boston, where the treaty was being signed, it wouldn't be the first time we'd seen a fae strolling through our small town in coastal Maine.

"I hope I'm selected," Jenny said.

Though all eligible women were entered into the lottery, the odds of Jenny being chosen to travel to the fae world to meet and possibly marry one of the nobles was pretty slim. Not because she didn't have a lot to offer. She was an incredible person, and she was pretty. But there had to be a billion women in the drawing, and only six would be chosen.

Personally, I was praying I *wouldn't* be selected. With an eight-year-old sister to raise after Mom died of cancer, I didn't have time for romance, even if the fae guys *were* hot.

Once chosen, the women would travel to the fae court, where they'd participate in a meet and greet with a bunch of fae lords, dukes, and a prince or two. No one would be forced to marry a fae guy, but the whole point of this was to match human women with a fae husband.

Anyone who didn't form an alliance within the three-month-long introductory period would return to our world with one million dollars. Only those who chose to marry could stay in the fae world. Something about mortals going out of their minds if they weren't 'bonded' to one of the fae. They'd been rather vague about that detail, and I hadn't looked into it since I wasn't interested in participating in the program.

It all sounded like something straight out of a reality TV show, with a fairytale twist. A year ago, if you'd told me fae existed, I would've laughed.

I wasn't laughing now.

"It'll take more than a decent haircut, makeup, and a nice dress for me to win a member of the fae aristocracy," she said, worrying her lip.

I put my arm around her waist and squeezed, sending her reassurance. "If you're picked, of course someone will fall in love with you."

"Order's up, Raven," Betty said, dropping two loaded plates onto the counter between the diner's bar and the kitchen. "Snap, snap," she added, though her eyes twinkled with humor. "Stop gossipin' and get workin'."

Eggs, bacon, and pancakes steamed on the platters, which the diner used as plates. Hearty food and lots of it was Betty's motto. I grabbed them and hustled over to booth two.

Then, with paper and pen in hand, and my heart pattering in my chest like a billion butterflies had taken flight, I hurried to booth three. The hostess had seated them, but they were in my section, so I'd serve them.

"Welcome to *Betty's Barnyard Biscuits*, where the bacon's thick, the eggs are farm raised, and the homemade biscuits are light and fluffy," I said in a cheery voice, spitting out the greeting Betty trained us to deliver. "Would you like to start with drinks?"

Don't stare at their gorgeousness, I told myself, but damn, it was hard. Up close, the fae were even more stunning than at a distance. The pictures on TV hadn't done them justice.

"Drinks?" one of them said in a deep, slightly accented voice that made my spine quiver.

"Coffee? Tea? We have fresh-squeezed orange juice or apple cider, if you'd prefer," I said.

Don't drool, either, I added to myself.

"I would like to try this coffee," the tallest of the bunch said. "I have heard much of it."

His hypnotic dark gaze met mine, and all I could picture were the elves in *Lord of the Rings*—only hotter. Long, dark hair threaded through with bits of silver hung past his shoulders. He could chip a diamond on his strong jawline. And his shoulders, outfitted in a dark gray tunic, spread forever, topping a muscular chest that narrowed to a trim waist.

My mouth went dry, and I guppy breathed. Would it be impolite to ask him to stand and turn in a slow circle so I could check out his thighs and butt? From what I'd seen on TV, these guys all wore snug black pants, and the view would be amazing.

"Our coffee is freshly brewed," I stuttered out, half in a trance.

He smoothed his hair off his shoulder, revealing an etched silver circlet high on his forehead. I didn't know how I'd missed it.

With his hair back, he revealed one of his distinctive, point-tipped ears. Other than their ears, the fae looked human. Well, if you ignored their height, clothing, and the glitter-spun hair everyone was copying, plus the slight shimmer surrounding them.

It's their magic, we were told.

They won't use it against us, someone else added.

I wouldn't mind this guy directing a bit of magic my way.

Chill, I told myself.

"Coffee it is," I said, struggling to remember what words were. "Would anyone else like something to drink?"

"Also coffee," the other three said in harmony, though I couldn't drag my gaze away from the tallest one long enough to look at them.

There was something about his face . . . I couldn't quite place why it felt off except, when I looked at him out of the corner of my eye, I swore his image wavered. Was he using some kind of magical mask to hide?

"Great. I'll be right back to take your order." I pressed a smile onto my face before pivoting and striding back behind the bar.

Shit. I could feel the weight of *his* gaze on my spine.

"Oh, God. Oh, God. Oh, God," Jenny said as I poured coffee into four cups. She sidled in close and leaned against my side. "You. Got. To. Speak. With. Them! Major envy right here, Rave. What are they like? Do they sound as dreamy as they look?"

"Even dreamier." Especially *him*. My hand literally

shook as I finished filling the final mug with coffee. It was all I could do not to slop it everywhere.

"Tell me. Tell me!"

"Later, chickie," I whispered. "Meet me in the break room after they leave."

I hefted the tray and eased around her, hurrying to the table to deliver their drinks. After tucking the empty tray beneath my arm, I lifted my pad of paper and pen. "Can I take your orders now?"

"What do you recommend . . . ?" The hot guy's gaze fell on my name tag. "Interesting name, *Raven*."

"Yeah. I can thank my dad for that." The dad I'd never known because he bailed on me and Mom before I was born. I forced a laugh. "At least he didn't call me Crow."

The fae guys all frowned.

Talk about a tough audience.

"We're known for our biscuits," I said, rushing to break the silence. "And the farmer delivers fresh eggs daily."

"I will order these . . . biscuits and eggs," the hot guy said. "How do you suggest they be prepared?"

"Over hard is my preference," I said. "But they're great scrambled too."

"I do like things hard." His voice came out smoother than honey, but he couldn't mean anything sexual by his comment. He lifted his cup. "This coffee is dee-lee-shoos."

My skin tingled, like he'd said *I* was delicious.

"We brew it fresh from beans we buy from a Costa

Rican supplier," I said.

He nodded slowly.

"Over hard eggs it is, then." I dragged my gaze away from his face and smiled at the other guys. "And what can I get you three?"

"We all want the same," one said, as if they couldn't think on their own or they admired the steamy guy so much they wanted to emulate him.

"Great," I said with a smile.

I put their orders in, but other than topping off their coffee, I had no excuse to linger at their table.

I *so* wanted to linger. Naw, I wanted to crawl into the hot guy's lap and wrap my legs around his waist. See if his full lips tasted as amazing as they looked.

I definitely needed to get out more. If I dated regularly, I wouldn't be so turned on by one guy's broody stare.

After they'd finished, I brought them their bill. Did the fae use debit cards? All I'd heard was that they lived in a mysterious kingdom right here on Earth, though it remained hidden behind magical spells.

They paid with cash, which wasn't a complete letdown. I hadn't expected gold coins I could bite on like in a movie.

Rising, they left the restaurant. None looked back, though I watched to see if the gorgeous guy would.

As I propped my side against the diner's bar, Jenny leaned against me, sighing along with me.

The hot fae guy took the sunshine with him when he left.

Chapter 2
Elion

"You play a dangerous game, my friend," Nuvian said as we strode down the street. Humans coming our way startled and jumped to the side, clearing a path. Nuvian bowed to an elderly female who tittered. He caught up to stride beside me after evading her clutches. "If you're not careful, you'll be burned."

I snorted. "That might be a nice change."

"You know what I mean."

Iolas and Ethar remained a few paces behind us, watching everything and listening to nothing. They were equally big, burly, and discrete. I couldn't have picked better fae to watch my back.

I hated needing guards. I could protect myself and had on all but one occasion, but after the incident that ruined my life, my liege lord had insisted. While I often did as I wished, not what he demanded, it was easier to relent in this one thing.

"I believe the human female saw that you projected a false image," Nuvian said.

"She didn't see through it, though, now did she?" I quirked up one eyebrow.

Why did he persist with this? I tamped down my irritation, having no wish to storm at my best friend and advisor.

"You don't know that," he said.

We turned a corner and walked downhill toward the beach.

"If she'd seen through my mask, she would've cringed or shrieked." Something I'd become used to.

"You don't repel everyone," Nuvian said.

I put my arm around his shoulder and forced a laugh. Two men walking from the other direction came to a standstill. Their eyes widened.

Iolas eased around me, putting himself between us as we passed.

They watched, their jaws agape.

"The next time we come here, we'll mask ourselves completely," I said. "If we look like every other human, no one will stare."

"Some like to be stared at."

"Not me," I grunted.

Never me.

It hadn't always been like this. I'd grown up confident in my looks and in my ability to attract others. With a crook of my finger and a quirk of my lips, I could make any female pant for my company.

Until that cold, dark night.

In the fae world, where all were universally gorgeous, though some were to a higher degree than others, my newly scarred appearance stood out. My fellow fae gaped. Snickered.

And no one looked at me with interest any longer.

I'd thought my appearance wouldn't make a difference, but the curse sunk deeper than my skin. I was doomed to a life without love.

Who needed an emotion like that? Not me. But sometimes, late at night, I ached to be with someone who'd see past the scars to the person I was inside.

"You'll hide for the next three months while the human females visit the kingdom," Nuvian said. "Promise me this."

"You do not need to protect me," I fumed, but he knew I wasn't truly angry. Everything he said was motivated by our friendship. He would do all he could to keep me from harm.

Especially the harm that could only be dealt by a woman.

"I'm forbidden to them, you know that," I said.

We stopped at the shore, staring toward the sea afloat with blocks of ice. Full winter was upon this world, making it easier to part the veil.

"Still," he said, "promise me you'll hide."

I grumbled but said nothing. Only lifted my arm to call the baishar. They burst from the sea, unrestrained, and plunged through the water to join us, their hides gleaming like bronze in full sunlight, their silvery manes dripping water. The three we'd summoned stopped in front of us, pawing the soft sand with their hooves and dipping their heads forward for pats.

Cupping the lead stallion's face, I eased around his horn, leaning forward to whisper. "Take me home, mighty one?"

He huffed, steam chugging from his nostrils.

I strode around to his side. The lingering wound on my leg savored the icy chill of the water. A leap, and I sat on the baishar's back, grasping a handful of his mane to keep from falling once he moved.

His fine silver wings unfurled as Iolas and Nuvian mounted the others.

We took flight, circling over the shore and heading out to sea.

The veil parted to admit us, and we left the human world for that of the fae.

I grumbled about our conversation. Nuvian was right to chastise me. Raven was lovely, but she'd never be mine.

I told myself it didn't matter. She wouldn't be among those chosen to solidify the treaty. I'd never see her again.

She'd bind with another in this world.

And when the human women arrived in the fae kingdom to fulfill their side of the agreement, I'd avoid the public areas of the castle where they'd linger. I'd only emerge from my rooms at night.

When they were gone, I'd be free to roam once again.

After that, I'd live out the rest of my days as the curse intended—a doomed shadow of a fae who'd never have love.

Chapter 3
Raven

"Lunch," I cried, lifting the paper bag as my little sister hurried out the front door. She was already late getting to the bus stop, but without lunch, she'd have to ask for food from the cafeteria. Or starve. If kids didn't have money to pay, the staff gave them leftovers from the day before. That food was bad enough the first time around, let alone the second.

I scooted after her and made her stop in the hall outside our apartment. After unzipping her backpack and dropping the bag inside, I hustled with her down the two flights of stairs.

We ripped out the front door and raced along the sidewalk to the corner.

The bus hovered beside the curb already, flashing lights on the top telling me the door was open.

"Come on," I shouted, breaking into a sprint, tugging Emme along with me.

If she missed the bus, I'd have to borrow the neighbor's car to take her the three miles to school. We could walk, but by the time I dropped her off, rushed home to change, then jogged to work, I'd be late.

I needed this job—desperately.

Betty might come across as sweet on the surface, but she had a steel spine. Like most, she had her rules, including being timely, and heaven help anyone who didn't obey. She didn't discipline us, but one sharp look would make even the Hulk's knees quake.

Fortunately, the bus driver must've seen us running down the sidewalk, because he waited.

We stopped by the open door. Stooping down in front of my half-sister, I stared into her dark green eyes so like mine and Mom's it hurt to see them. I tousled the blonde hair she got from her dad.

"Be good today," I said.

"I will." Emme had been withdrawn since Mom died two months ago, but who could blame her? Sixteen years older than her eight, I was the sister who'd lived three hundred miles away. I went to college, though I was late starting because I had to save after I moved out. Sure, I helped Mom with Emme until I left, and I always brought her great gifts when I came home for the holidays, but I hadn't been a big part of her life until Mom's diagnosis.

"All aboard," the bus driver called. He wiggled the door handle.

"Love you, Em." I kissed her cheek, then straightened, urging her up the steps. "I'll see you later. Have a great day at school!"

"Bye, Raven," she called as she stomped up the steps. She dropped into one of the front seats and pressed her palm against the glass.

The bus took off, and with tears stinging the back of my eyes, I waved and kept a smile on my face until it turned the corner, disappearing from view.

My heavy sigh slipped out. I loved my sister. I was grateful I could give her a decent life. But it wasn't easy stepping into a parental role at twenty-four.

Turning to head back home, I froze.

A wolf stood on the sidewalk a hundred feet away. Its gray ruff ruffled in the breeze, and its dark eyes appeared to glow.

It was the most gorgeous creature I'd seen in my life.

When I was little, I told Mom I dreamed about wolves. In my dreams, they were my friends, and I ran with them. She seemed so spooked by my comment I never brought it up again. As I grew older, I stopped dreaming about them, which made me sad. I missed them.

This wolf was bigger than my fantasy friends, almost four-foot-tall at his shoulders. With his long fangs and big, clawed paws, I got the feeling he could rip almost anything apart.

His thick coat gleamed like polished silver. His tail swooped back and forth slowly. If I stooped down and held out my hand, would he run over and lick it?

Because seeing a wolf in a rural Maine town was so out of place, I literally rubbed my eyes.

When I opened them again, the wolf was gone.

"It was your tears messing with your vision," I whispered as I remained frozen in place. "It wasn't an actual wolf. Especially a silver one gleaming like polished metal."

As I started walking again, I ran through the possibilities to explain what I'd seen. "It was a big, silver dog. Its eyes didn't *really* glow. That was a reflection of the sunlight."

Other than the rare moose or porcupine, wild creatures didn't just stride through small towns like mine. If wolves still existed in this part of the U.S., they lived in the deep woods of northwestern Maine.

My phone alarm hummed in my back pocket. Shit. It was time for me to leave for work.

Forget the wolf—*dog.*

Racing back to our apartment, I dressed and gathered up my things, then grabbed my key off the table by the front door. I paused and stared at the photo hanging on the wall, tracing my finger down Mom's right cheek.

A stranger took this picture of the three of us when we splurged on a whale watching tour two summers ago. I'd come home to visit for a full week instead of my rare long weekend.

The wind blew, and Mom had insisted we put on our jackets. *No need to be chilly, sweeties*, she'd said. In the picture, our hoods were tied snugly beneath our chins, but the wind still tried to steal our hair, tugging it from beneath the nylon fabric.

This was before Mom's cancer diagnosis. Before she lost her gorgeous brown hair and got rail thin from the cancer eating her up inside. When her green eyes still sparkled with life.

I braced my arm on the wall and smiled, though it came out shaky. It hurt to breathe. "Miss you, Mom. So much. I'm taking good care of Emme. I promise."

It hadn't been easy to quit college and move back home eight months ago, but I'd do it again in a heartbeat. Quitting meant I'd been here to take Mom to her treatments. To hold her hand when the pain was so bad that my usually stoic mom cried.

I'd been at her bedside when she pulled in her last breath.

Cancer took her much too fast.

Straightening, I swiped away my tears. They kept falling, but that was okay. I'd love her forever, and it was crap that she was taken from us so soon. But I'd never denied myself the chance to mourn.

Chapter 4
Elion

I lied to Nuvian. Rather than hide in my rooms while the kingdom prepared for the human brides, I mounted my favorite baishar and snuck back through the veil.

I told myself I only needed to see her one more time. I wouldn't speak to her, and I certainly wouldn't touch her.

I'd watch. Ensure she was safe. Then I'd leave and never seek her out again. I'd take a taste, not devour the full meal.

When I reached the human world, I . . . changed. I'd not only been cursed with a scarred face and the inability to find love, but I'd also been turned into something unheard of in the fae world for generations.

A despised shifter. Despised by my people, that is, but no longer by me. I relished my ability to seamlessly turn into someone other than myself. To run through the woods. To sniff the musty, vibrant odors most missed.

It didn't take long to find Raven. I watched as she escorted the smaller version of herself into a big glowing orange vehicle. It left, and she turned.

Despite the magical cloak I'd spread over my form to disguise me from view, she *saw* me. How was that possible?

Even more interesting, she held out her hand like she wanted to touch me.

I ached to feel her fingers running through my ruff, to nudge her side, to whine with pleasure while she stroked me.

It wasn't possible, and the sooner I accepted that, the better.

When she closed her eyes, I faded from view. I needed to return to the kingdom. My guards would notice I was gone, and they'd seek me. After what happened, my family was wise to keep a close eye on me, though I strained against their bindings.

Still, I didn't leave. I continued to watch her, following her with the soft pads of my wolfish feet. She hurried to her home, and I hid outside, ignoring a cat who hissed on the top step. Felines saw unlike any other. My snarl spooked it, and it bolted down the sidewalk and around the corner.

I watched her door, telling myself I did this to protect her. She didn't realize how thin the veil was between my world and hers. She didn't realize how easy it would be for someone to grab her. If she disappeared, did she have family who'd miss her other than the child?

She hurried out of the building, ran down the steps, and raced along the sidewalk.

Slinking, I followed, feeling stupider by the minute. I was a member of the fae aristocracy, fifth in line for the throne. I didn't need to skulk after human females. Whatever her fate held, it would unfold whether I watched her or not.

Leaving felt like the wrong thing to do, however.

When a tall, thin male stepped out behind her, his focus solely on her, I discovered why I'd lingered.

After shooting a nervous glance over her shoulder, she clutched her bag and broke into a jog.

He picked up speed, keeping pace as she darted around a corner.

I drew closer, hovering a claw's reach from his spine.

Flames licked through my heart. I wanted to leap on him and slam him onto the ground. Teach him with my fangs and claws to never frighten her again.

He reached into his pocket and pulled a knife. The blade slicked free. Rushing forward, he grabbed Raven's hair, wrapping the long strands around his hand.

The knife lifted . . .

A roar ripped from my throat, and he shot a look of terror in my direction.

Raven stomped down hard on his foot. When he released her with a bellow, she turned and raced down the sidewalk.

My cloak of magic melted, and I let him see what was coming. He was the one being stalked by a true predator. His breath caught, and he turned to run, his arms flailing.

His knife clattered to the sidewalk as I leaped onto his back.

We went down in a cluster of puny human limbs and furious, bristling wolf. I caught his neck and pinned him to the pavement.

He didn't stand a chance. Though I was sorely tempted, I didn't kill him. He deserved it and so much more. But someone would notice, and this wouldn't slip past the kingdom's attention. They'd know who it was. They'd know I left without my guard.

Frustration bristled the fur on my spine, but I released the human and backed away.

He rose. Whimpering, he raced across the street and took off in the opposite direction.

My magical cloak restored, I sought Raven, but she'd fled from view.

Had she seen her protector?

I trotted toward the diner, catching up as she opened the door and hurried inside.

Confident she was safe for now, I crossed the road and slunk into the shadows of a two-story building.

The slant of the sun told me I couldn't remain much longer. My magic was limited in the human world, and I'd spent much of it crafting my invisibility cloak.

I growled, wishing I could remain here until Raven was once more secure inside her home, though I doubted the human male would stalk her again.

I lingered, watching the diner until the sun slanted across me.

Turning, I ran through town and to the beach where I shifted back to my fae form.

I stood near the water and called my baishar. And called him a second time when he didn't heed my summons. The creatures had free will, but we gave them treats to keep them eager to respond to our call.

Frowning, I paced along the beach, my boots crunching on small stones. Waves sped up the slope and tried to grab hold of me, but I fought them. I wouldn't be sucked into the sea's empty embrace.

A sound behind me sent me spinning. A baishar splashed through the water in my direction. Not the one I always used, but one I recognized from the pack.

He stood still, blowing as I approached and leaped onto his spine.

Taking flight, he soared toward the slice in the veil, his tail swishing. It didn't take long to reach the outskirts of the kingdom. He flew over the forest, his hooves grazing across leaves on the tops of the tallest trees.

I sensed something watching in the dense woods below, but when I leaned over to look, I didn't see anything of concern.

As I settled back on the baishar, my spine twitched.

The baishar landed outside the castle's stables, and I dismounted, patting the creature's neck.

A nymph ran from the stable to take the mount. She'd cool him down and feed him the nectar the creature craved.

I strode toward where the woods crept right up to the

side of the stables. Staring into the forest, I sent out a seeking spell.

What are you, and what do you want with me?

The spell hit something. It snapped back and smacked me hard enough that some might've been knocked off their feet.

I stiffened my legs and held my position.

A snarl ripped through me, and whatever attacked slunk backward into the deepest part of the forest.

It couldn't hide from me. I raced into the woods, following its narrow trail, determined to discover what watched, and who had sent it.

I reached the place where an odd scent hung in the air; a damp, musty smell that burned my sinuses.

A snap behind me sent me spinning.

Someone rushed at me, and I was taken to the ground.

Chapter 5
Raven

A guy had chased me. He'd caught me and who knows what he would've done to me. He'd had a knife!

But something scared him. I hadn't stopped to see what it was; I'd bolted, running the rest of the way to the diner.

I leaned against the back of the door in the hallway outside the kitchen, my heart slamming in my chest, my breathing ragged. I couldn't stop shaking.

Jenny swooped into the kitchen and raced toward me. "They're doing the drawing." She frowned at my sweaty face but linked her arm through mine and dragged me through the kitchen and out into the main dining area to stand beneath the flat screen TV mounted above the bar.

"Let me put my bag in the break room," I said, my voice one big quaver.

"It's happening now," Jenny danced in place. "You can do that later."

The surrounding customers went silent as the Earth Ambassador to the Fae Court appeared on the screen.

Even Betty scooted from the kitchen to watch, wiping her hands on her starched apron.

I dropped my pack on the floor and swiped my sweaty hair out of my eyes.

"Welcome," the Ambassador said in with a heavy accent. "I am so honored to be with you today." He held his clasped hands in front of his chest. "First, I wish to thank all you lovely women who have entered for a chance to compete in this most unusual event."

"We didn't, not really," I whispered. They hadn't exactly *made* us enter, but if we were single, okay with marrying a fae dude, and between the ages of twenty and thirty, our names were thrown into the lottery.

"Shh," Jenny said. Grinning, she linked her arm through mine.

"Hurry it up," a guy called out from behind me. A couple of the others laughed. "Well, my coffee's cold, and no one's going to top it off as long as they're watching the damn TV."

Leaving Jenny, I grabbed the pot off the burner and poured him some with a smile.

"Thanks, darlin'," he said, adding cream. His gaze remained glued on the screen.

After returning the pot to the burner, I stood beside Jenny again, leaning back against the counter.

"It's okay if you're not picked," I said. This event was all she had talked about over the past few months. She was such a sweet person, I hated to see her disappointed.

"Once chosen, the fae will collect you," the Ambassador said. "You'll be given time to say goodbye to any family, but don't worry about packing. The fae will provide for all your needs once you arrive in the kingdom."

"I heard they'll outfit each woman with gorgeous gowns," Jenny said with an excited shiver. "They'll assign servants to help us with our hair and makeup. Can you imagine?" She hugged my arm. "Whoever is chosen will be dressed like royalty."

That wasn't my thing, but it sure was Jenny's. I was more a jeans and t-shirt kinda gal.

"Without further ado," the Ambassador said. "It's time to announce the young ladies who will travel to the fae kingdom to form alliances to cement our new treaty. As you know, the king's wizard did the selection herself, ensuring the drawing was honest and fair." He lifted his hand and a golden cylinder with sparkling silver tassels floated into the room.

"Cool," Jenny breathed. Her clammy hand tightened on my arm, and she scrunched her shoulders up into her neck. "Hold me."

Caught up in her enthusiasm, I released a giddy laugh and put my arm around her waist.

The Ambassador plucked the cylinder from the air and pulled on a tiny gold ring dangling from the bottom, unfurling the scroll. He leaned forward, squinting. "The first name is Bettina Blake." He added a code, the unique identifier we'd each received when we'd entered, then flashed a toothy smile our way.

"Not me," Jenny said, clasping her hands beneath her chin. "Five left. Cylinder number two? Don't fail me now, baby!"

Another cylinder floated toward the Ambassador, and he grabbed it, tugging down the ring. He yelled out the name.

"Ugh, not me," Jenny gnawed on her fingernail.

Another cylinder and a third name. Then the fourth and fifth.

"Shit, there's only one spot left," Jenny said, turning teary eyes my way. "What if I'm not picked?"

"You wait for the next round?" Though there'd been no indication anyone else in the fae kingdom would seek a human bride.

She latched onto my hand. "I can deal. I can. It's just—"

"And the final contestant . . ." the Ambassador said as the last cylinder floated into view. He grinned. "Should I draw this out, ladies?"

"Don't," Jenny whispered. "Please."

"Could I get more coffee?" an older guy sitting at the bar called out. "At this rate, we'll be here all day. I need to get to work, and I'm useless without my two cups."

I left Jenny and grabbed the pot, filling his cup with a ready smile.

"Thanks," he grumbled. "At least one of you is working today."

"We're just excited," I said.

"You don't seem as eager as Jenny."

"I'm caring for my younger sister," was my ready answer. "Remember? Mom died."

Everyone knew everyone in my small town.

He reached across the bar, patting my shoulder. "She was a good woman, your mom. I was really sorry to hear cancer took her."

"Thanks," I said, my eyes tearing. I sniffed and wiped them away.

"It's okay to dream," he said. "We all do it."

Would it be wrong to admit that deep within my heart and only late-late at night, I'd wondered what it would be like if *I* was chosen? It was wrong. I needed to be here for Emme. I shouldn't dream of marrying a member of the fae nobility.

"Just remember that, Raven," the older guy said. He scratched his gray head. "Your mom wouldn't want you holing up in her apartment, living only to raise your little sister."

"There'll be time for me later. She's only eight." She was grieving, just like me.

"And the final name is . . ." the Ambassador called out behind me.

I glanced toward the TV. It didn't matter. It was best for me to remain grounded here on plain old Earth.

"Raven Wilder," the Ambassador crowed.

I stared at the TV, stunned.

"Guess life is choosing for you," the old guy said, but I couldn't look at him. There was no way I could drag my gaze from the screen.

"It's a mistake. It's a mistake!" I whispered. He hadn't called my name.

But the number he announced matched. I'd memorized it. No clue why.

Jenny latched onto my arms. "Way to go, girl! Wow, wow, wow." She pressed for a smile that didn't quite reach her eyes, but I could tell she was happy for me. She took the coffeepot from my limp fingers before I dropped it and placed it on the burner.

"I can't . . ." I said, my voice coming out weak. "I need to stay here for Emme."

"I'll take care of her." Jenny tugged me into a hug, whispering in my ear. "Go. Win the heart of a fae duke, then send for Emme. I imagine they'll let her come live with you if you stay there."

"I don't want a fae duke."

"Then lure in a prince." She frowned. "Assuming there is a prince."

"I need to remain here." Despite the old guy's nudge, work and caring for my half-sister was more than enough excitement for me.

My gaze was drawn to the big picture window. On the other side of the street, something gleamed. I squinted and bit off my gasp.

The silver wolf was back, and he was watching me.

"Go flirt with fae guys but keep your heart secure," Jenny said. "Then when the three-month period is over, you can return here with a million dollars."

Who'd turn down an offer like that?

"You know I'll take good care of Emme." Jenny's soft

gaze met mine. "This is an opportunity of a lifetime. I'll handle things here. You won't be gone long."

I looked out the window, but the wolf was gone. I was imagining this, right? There was no other explanation.

Shaking my head, I dismissed the creature from my mind.

Jenny was right. None of the fae guys would fall for me.

And I'd make sure I didn't fall for any of them.

Chapter 6
Raven

The fae had come for me.

My heart in my throat, I waved from the back seat of the black SUV until I couldn't see my half-sister standing on the front steps beside my cousin.

Turning to face forward, I sucked in a jagged breath. My chest hurt. My eyes kept watering.

There was no way in hell I wanted to do this. Marry some unknown fae guy? No thanks. I didn't need romance or magic in my life.

I just wanted to raise my sister.

The driver took the vehicle beyond the outskirts of town, weaving it along the coast. Saying nothing, the fae man in the passenger seat stared out the window.

Sunlight winked on the water to my right, and evergreens spiked toward the sky. I loved the coast, the salty spray, and the crisp, heavy scent of the ocean filling the air. In the summer, I sat on the rocky shore and soaked up the rays. In the winter, when there wasn't much snow, I bundled up and walked as far as my legs could take me.

Mom used to come with me.

My heart ached, but there wasn't anything I could do about it except convince our government and the fae king that I was giving this a solid effort, then scurry back home where I belonged.

Twenty minutes later, the driver pulled the vehicle onto a dirt lane on our right. I'd been out this way a few times. This path only led to the beach, certainly not to a transportation center.

"Where are we going?" I wasn't exactly afraid, though my thudding heart suggested otherwise.

"We are almost there," the driver said.

"We're going for a walk on the beach?" I was only half-joking.

"We travel to the fae kingdom from here," he insisted, totally serious.

"There's nothing down this road but a parking lot and the beach."

They said nothing.

The vehicle bumped along the road, and if it was dark out, I'd be sweating, and my pulse would be raging in my throat. I'd be looking for weapons ...

Daylight didn't mean I was any safer, but worst-case scenario, I could run.

I'd brought my pepper spray. I carefully eased the small cannister out of my bag I'd dropped on the seat beside me and palmed the pink cartridge. When a girl lived in a city, she learned things.

My tense belly eased when we left the woods and emerged out into the small lot above the beach. Other vehicles waited, fae escorts milling around outside the row of completely black SUVs.

The driver parked our SUV beside the others and shut off the engine.

"Do we wait here for . . . another ride?" I asked, unbuckling. I thought of returning my pepper spray to my bag but decided to hold off on that. My instincts were going haywire, and they suggested there was no harm in remaining on guard.

"We travel from here," the driver said, opening his door.

"How?" I called as he stepped outside.

The other one turned in his seat, and his teal eyes sparkled. "Magic," he whispered before exiting the car.

Huh. Since the fae revealed they'd traveled among us on occasion, there'd been wild speculation about them. I heard they could use glamour to mask their appearance, and they must've done that, or someone would've talked about their height and pointy ears. But only a few speculated about their magic. The assumption was they couldn't do much with it. Or it didn't work here as well as it did in their kingdom.

Unease bloomed inside me, but I shrugged it off. I'd learn all about them once I arrived in the kingdom. Hell, maybe I could sell my story to a supermarket magazine when I returned. *Raven reveals scandalous details about the fae!* That would be a hoot. I'd take mental notes while I was there.

I grabbed my bag and got out of the car.

Doors opened, and women emerged from the other SUVs. I'd seen them on TV over the past few days, so I recognized them. Everyone was desperate for information about the chosen few.

They started clustering together on the walkway beyond the front of the vehicles, so I hitched my backpack higher on my shoulder and joined them.

Three white ladies, including me, with various hair colors, styles, and body shapes. An Asian woman about my age with a medium frame like mine, plus a dark-skinned woman, as if those running the program had made sure to include other races than plain old white bread.

We nodded to each other, but no one made introductions. Perhaps that would come later, once we'd settled in the castle.

Which . . . A freakin' castle? We'd been told we'd stay there and attend various functions that would introduce us to a wide range of fae nobility. If we hit it off with any of them, we could pursue more. The idea was to mix our two people to ensure we both had a vested interest in maintaining the peace.

"Is it always this cold here?" one of the women said in a crisp British accent. She wrapped her arms around her waist, but really, I could've told her if she wanted to stay warm in a November Maine, she needed a coat. Mittens. Not a thin dress with no sleeves. She looked great with her blonde hair bluntly cut to brush along her jawline, but I didn't regret my jeans, tee, and heavy hooded sweatshirt. I could stuff my hands into the pockets.

"Yes, it is," I said when no one else spoke. "It's winter. It'll warm up by May if you want to hang around to try it out."

Her pale pink lips thinned. "I'm going to marry one of the fae. I certainly won't be returning to this place." Her blue eyes took in the evergreens marching down to the gray beach, plus the few cottages built well above the rocky coastline. I bristled at her tone, but when I caught appreciation in her gaze, not derision, my bubble of irritation burst. "It's lovely here; I'll give you that. But it's so rural. We've barely seen anyone since we left Portland."

"That's the beauty of this part of Maine," I said, revising my opinion of her. She might come off snooty, but maybe she was just as nervous as me. "It's not developed."

Our fae escorts had gathered in the parking lot. When I started to ask what was going on, they strode toward us.

"How will we travel to the kingdom?" the Asian woman asked in such a firm voice that it almost came out sharp. She traced her fingers down a band of her long, dark hair. Her nod took me in. "I'm Nashio, by the way. I'm from San Francisco."

"Raven. From here, and I'm not sure how we'll get there."

"It is time to depart, ladies," a fae man with hair blacker than the darkest night said. "If you would join us on the beach?"

"So, this is weird," a redhead said, leaning her shoulder against mine. "I'm Bettina. Call me Betts." Her sharp brown gaze remained on the fae men as they left the lot and walked down toward the sea. "I'm not striding into the Maine ocean on a November day, not even on a dare."

I snorted. "I'm with you. Maybe on New Year's Day and after a pitcher of mimosas. Right now, we'll be lucky if the water's fifty degrees."

The guys stopped above the line of waves and turned back to us.

"Come on," Betts said, following them down to the beach.

The rest of us looked at each other, shrugged, and joined them.

The dark-haired fae guy released a low, guttural cry.

One of the women tittered, ending the sound with a slap of her hand over her mouth.

Splashes erupted from the water, and I gaped as four unicorns pulling a carriage straight out of a fairytale danced toward us.

One of the fae guys joined them in the water. He stroked the lead unicorn and urged the creature to leave the water. The others paced beside the first.

"Holy fuck," Betts said. "It's . . . I've never seen anything like it."

"Amazing," Nashio breathed.

A fae opened the door on the side of the carriage and waved toward the inside. "Ladies."

Gulping, I walked with the other women. We climbed inside, settling on black velvet cushions.

"The ocean . . ." the British woman said. I got the feeling she was rarely flustered, but color rode high in her pale cheeks. "We'll travel into it?"

I shrugged and peered out the window on my side.

The door shut, and the creatures turned. They galloped into the water, then lifted off.

"Fuck, we're flying," Betts shrieked. "What's keeping us from dropping?"

"It's like Santa's sleigh," the woman with dark skin said, her brown eyes sparkling. "Magic is holding us aloft. I'm Rhaelyn, by the way."

"Madison," the British woman said.

"And I'm Crystal," the last white woman said. She dipped her head forward, and her blonde hair woven into a tight braid flipped across her shoulder to the front. She shoved it back. "This is quite the trip, huh?"

We all peered out the windows, unable to look away.

I wasn't sure when we passed the veil, the barrier between our world and theirs, but soon, we were floating over a forest.

We touched down onto a cobblestone driveway, and the unicorn's hooves clicked as they carried us up toward the castle.

"I've died and gone to Disney," Rhaelyn said.

Crystal released a nervous laugh. "I hope there's running water. I'm not into bathing in streams."

We passed big flowerbeds with pale pink flowers. The forest marched right up to the lawn, made up of tall, spindly trees with deep purple leaves. A pale purple bird bigger than my head landed on top of one of the trees and studied us.

With a harsh caw, it lifted off, flying away quickly.

The carriage stopped in front of a series of granite steps leading up to the stone castle, and the door opened.

"If you'll follow me," the fae guy who'd helped us into the carriage called out. "We'll soon get you settled in your rooms. You can refresh yourselves, then join us in the main parlor for a light repast."

"Repast," Crystal mouthed. Her lips twitched and humor shone in her eyes. "I think I need a stiff drink."

"Me too," I said.

"Me three," Rhaelyn added.

Betts turned a raised-eyebrow look my way. "Holy shit."

My laugh barked out. "Totally."

We'd arrived in the fae kingdom.

Chapter 7
Elion

I flung myself to the side before the flazire could impale me with a claw. Landing hard, I rolled, coming up to a crouch.

The wiry demon made of sinew and sparse tan fur, with clawed hands and feet, tipped its head back and shrieked.

I didn't have time to wonder why it was here, because it hurtled itself toward me.

Others slunk from the woods, creeping in to flank it and surround me.

Getting away was my top priority, but they'd give chase on the trail. I had to eliminate a few of them, or I wouldn't stand a chance.

All I had for defense was the stick by my feet, but it would have to do. I grabbed it and tested its weight, pleased it felt green and not rotted.

When one darted toward me, its unearthly scream making my skin crawl, I stabbed out with the stick, hitting it in the right eye. Spinning, I tumbled to the side, barely avoiding being eviscerated by a swipe of its claws. It spun, wailing and clutching its face. A pop and he disappeared, returning to the underworld.

One down. Eight to go.

I shifted into my wolf, a creature I'd despised when I was cursed with him. I'd come to appreciate him since then. We had an uneasy truce.

Rip them, I said in my mind.

He grunted, eager. As far as I knew, he could understand my thoughts, but he'd never responded verbally. Only in impressions that were often too vague for me to interpret.

Leaping, he took a demon down to the ground, his fangs going for the creature's throat. A shake, and he flung himself off the demon and onto another. The mauled beast from the underworld released a pop and disappeared, sent back to where it had come from.

I didn't often give him control of our wolf body. It felt wise to keep him on a tight leash. Now, I gave him free rein, and I savored what he did with the opportunity.

Three more pops, and we were dealing with four.

I took back my body, shifting quickly to me, and hefted the stick.

The remaining demons attacked at once, slamming into my back and sides. I dove forward, tumbling, and came to my feet, dismayed to see five more slunk from the woods and into the meadow.

This was too much like the night when I was cursed.

Her minions had trapped me in a ravine, and only my sword saved my life.

She'd already taken everything from me, though I didn't know why. Why bother to send them after me again? That night, they caught me and carried me to her where she refused to say a thing to me other than the harsh, grating spell she cast that wrapped a curse so tight around me, I could barely breathe. She released me after that, and despite seeking her to force her to undo her spell, I'd been unable to find her.

If I thought the demons planned to take me to her again, I'd be tempted to let them do it. But today, they appeared more eager to kill than capture me.

The ones scrambling up my back and sides tried to weigh me down, so I'd fall to the ground, but I whipped my arms out, flinging them off me.

While they snarled and scrambled to their feet to attack again, I raced for the woods, hitting the trail at a dead run. I ran as fast as I could, leaping over roots and downed trees blocking the path. Thorn bushes snagged my clothing and pierced my flesh. Some whipped my face, snagging on the scars left by *her*. With blood streaming down my face, I kept going. If I didn't escape them, it was over.

After she'd cursed me, I hadn't cared if I lived or died, but now I had a thread of a purpose, something keeping me from giving up altogether.

Raven.

I was stupid to place hope of ending this curse on a slip of a human, but there it was. I sensed something pure and giving within her. It reached out to the soft side of me that I believed was ground to dust by *her* actions.

Raven might just be enough . . .

But if I died here, there would be no chance.

The demons gave chase, shrieking loud enough to wake the dead. They kept even with me in the woods, others joining in on the hunt, galloping behind me on the trail.

They *played* with me, and there wasn't a damn thing I could do about it.

My heart had turned into a ball of fire in my chest, and my breathing was a hoarse wheeze.

One squealed as its claws raked out, dragging down my left shoulder and arm. Pain burst through me as my skin parted. Blood poured from the wound, dripping down my flank and thigh. If I didn't get help, I'd bleed out. They'd overpower me and take me to the ground and devour me. No one would find anything but scraps of fabric and bones.

I spun and struck out with the stick, hitting the demon hard with the pointed end. It pierced the creature's skin, and the beast bled a sickly yellow trail only a shade darker than its soiled mustard skin.

It tumbled sideways, crashing into the brush and rolling in the dead leaves. Its cries echoed around us as I pivoted and fled.

Others approached. Whoever sent them was determined to make sure I didn't make it back to the castle alive.

They rushed at me from all sides, one slamming

against my waist. Its claws and spiked tail scrambled across my back, and I was grateful I wore a tundeer vest. The creature's claws slid off, unable to find purchase on the thick, nearly impervious material.

I flung it away, and it landed hard in the thorny bushes, releasing shrieks of pain.

Its cries were echoed by others, and I could tell they scrambled to get ahead of me. They'd wait on the path and with so many, there would be no escape.

I hated this would be my end. I'd thought my life would mean . . . something. Or that I'd find love in someone other than my deceased mother.

Even my younger sister scorned me. She'd chosen her place in the court, cementing it with her disdain toward me, even though this meant turning her back on her only surviving family.

With blood streaming down my face and back, I found the strength for a burst of speed. I flung myself from the woods, hitting the hard-packed dirt outside the stable.

They followed, exposing themselves to sunlight. Their skin smoldered, but still they only shrieked and gave chase.

Roaring to my feet, I bolted for the castle. I stumbled across the gardens, nearly falling on hedges to reach the front.

Though I didn't look, I felt the demons melting backward into the woods. If they were wise, they'd avoid being seen. Challenging me was one thing. Taking on the full guard would prove lethal. They were universally hated by the fae.

A large carriage sat in the drive, but I paid it no mind. I took the steps two at a time, feral in my determination to get inside the dubious sanctuary. At least there, I had a few loyal guards and friends. They'd help when no one else would.

I tripped on the top step and slammed forward onto my hands and knees.

The human brides had arrived, and they gaped at me. One bit off a shriek with a hand clamped over her mouth. They backed away, whimpering.

Without my glamour, I was nothing but a bloody beast kneeling at their feet.

I could handle the shame and embarrassment. I could.

Until my gaze met Raven's.

Chapter 8
Raven

When a fae guy tripped on the stairs and dropped to his knees at my feet, one of the other women shrieked. All of them backed away as if he had just projectile vomited in front of us.

I stared in horror at the blood trickling down his face, more concerned that he was injured than in the thick network of scars on his face that continued down his neck and beneath his tunic. Tears and stains covered his clothing, making him look like he'd tangled with a cheetah.

One of the other women snickered.

"Graceful, he is not," she said with a laugh.

My face overheated. I wasn't responsible for anyone else's actions, but I still felt embarrassed by my association with them. When Mom had chemo, she lost her hair. We went to the supermarket once, and someone laughed, and that just about killed me.

"Are you okay?" I asked him, holding out my hand to help him rise. "You're bleeding."

He looked up at me, and for just a second, despair flashed through his eyes. It tugged at something deep inside me. Rumors said fae guys could do magic, that if you locked eyes with them, they'd enthrall you. You'd never be free. You'd slowly lose your sense of self until nothing remained but him and the demands he'd make of you.

I had a feeling this guy could get me to do almost anything, and that scared me. I wasn't here for emotions. I wasn't here to fall in love.

He brushed aside my hand and stood. His gaze penetrated mine, and I suspected he was waiting for me to join in with the others, to mock him.

"Are you all right?" I asked again. "That was quite a fall."

"I am."

His low, deep voice made my knees go melty. Was he one of the prospective bridegrooms? If so, it might be harder to avoid hooking up with one of them than I'd thought.

"We need to go inside." Betts was tugging on my sleeve. Her voice lifted. "Everyone is going inside, Raven."

"Yeah," I said, flicking my hand in her direction. "Be right with you."

His lips twisted in a sneer. "Yes, little bride, you must go inside."

The words popped from me before I could voice them. "Will you be seeking a bride?"

Why in the hell was I asking? I hadn't come here to

get married. I needed to return to my sister. For all I knew, he was already taken.

A stab went through my heart at the thought of him kissing a gorgeous fae woman, his wife—the woman he'd love for eternity. It shouldn't matter.

"I am not," he said with a sneer. He leaned close, and his words tickled down my spine. "Do not look at me or speak with me again."

Before I could do more than sputter, he'd strode around me and entered the building.

"Asshole," Betts hissed. "You were nice, and he treated you like shit."

"Yeah," I said softly. My belly twisted, and now, I felt embarrassed for myself. I shouldn't have asked him a personal question like that.

My gaze was drawn to a fae guy sitting about twenty feet from us on the stone decking. His face remained hidden in the building's shade, but the weight of his stare hit me like a brick in the face. Chills rippled across my skin, and I hugged my waist with my arms.

"Come on." Betts shot the guy a glare. "Stop gaping, buddy," she called out. "You're creeping us out." Her arm went around my shoulders, and she guided me through the enormous carved wooden door and into the dark interior. "Whoa. Check out the foyer."

Even what should've been a simple room overwhelmed me. My entire apartment would fit inside. The ceiling rose at least three stories above us, and they'd painted it with cherubs and . . . demons? I wasn't sure, but the red guys cavorting with the cherubs had horns and lips spread wide to reveal their fangs.

A ginormous staircase rose to the first landing before splitting and continuing up to the second floor. Tiers of stairs continued above that, and I assumed each level could be accessed from this room, though there had to be other staircases scattered about the multi-acre palace.

I sensed . . . something I couldn't define. Like someone watched me, though that would be creepy. Instead, the attention felt like a warm caress. I wanted to close my eyes and drink in the feeling.

Swiften up, Raven. This was the fae kingdom, a place full of magic. If I was noticing something, I needed to consider the creep factor, not just how tantalizing the sensation might be.

Movement on the third story drew my eye, and I swore . . . Nah. It couldn't be the guy from out front.

A tall, stately fae woman walked calmly down the stairs and stopped in the center of the foyer. I focused on her, not the odd feeling.

"Welcome, ladies. I am Camile, and I will be your host while you visit the fae kingdom." She dipped forward in a shallow bow, then swept her arm toward an open archway to our left. "Shall we go to the front parlor to wait until your rooms are ready?" Turning, she strode into the parlor, her pale blue gown brushing the tops of her golden shoes.

Nashio grinned at me. "This place is amazing, isn't it?"

"Is that gold leaf on the walls?" Crystal asked, leaning forward to pick at it with her nail.

A guard flanking the entrance cleared his throat, and Crystal shot him a sheepish look before scurrying after Camile with us following.

Before I entered the parlor, I squinted up to the third-floor landing. While I didn't see anybody there, I swore someone watched. I shook off the feeling and left the foyer.

"Sit, please," Camile said, waving to the many sofas spotting this equally big room. Her attention narrowed on me like I was an unruly child caught misbehaving.

What? I didn't do anything.

"This is a parlor?" Betts asked. "What kind of entertaining do they do here?"

"All kinds," Camile said, though with a kind smile. "You'll soon see how busy the aristocracy is here, and not only with government-related duties. We regularly host soirees, balls, intimate cocktail hours, and too many other functions to mention. You'll participate in all of them until you've met your match and settled into your new life here in the kingdom."

Talk about daunting. I knew we were expected to attend multiple events, but I hadn't realized we'd step into the shoes of a fae princess.

I perched on the edge of a floral-patterned loveseat and crossed my legs at the ankles. Fire crackled in the big stone fireplace to my left, the face climbing all the way to the three-story ceiling.

"As your host, it's my job to escort you through the

process," Camile said. "Though other staff will be assigned to your entourage for the duration of your stay."

"Entourage?" Betts whispered, rolling her eyes.

Camile lifted her eyebrows at Betts, who slunk back against the sofa cushions and pressed her fingers over her mouth.

"Today will be the simplest day of your stay, so prepare yourselves," Camile continued. "I suggest you rest once you reach your rooms. Soon, your full staff will arrive to help ready you for the first events of the afternoon. A snack will be brought to your rooms at that time, and I recommend you eat well." Her thin lips pursed. "Please don't embarrass yourself—or me—by overeating in public."

Eat in the room, not where anyone could watch, then. Got it.

Camile turned to someone entering the parlor. "Ah, here they are. As your name is called, please go with your escort." Her lips spread in a neutral smile again. "I'll meet up with you shortly before the first event to give you some last-minute instructions. I'm confident you'll make me proud." Her words held a slight warning, but I wasn't going to do anything stupid. I'd behave and leave this place as soon as I could.

The other women left one-by-one, as they were called, until it was just me and Camile in the parlor.

Camile frowned at the staff member standing in the archway, and the petite fae woman slunk back into the foyer. She rose when I did, but her hand snapped out, her bony fingers digging into my arm, holding me back. "Just a word, if you will . . . I apologize. I don't recall your name."

"I'm Raven."

"Ah, yes, *Raven*. Such an unusual name."

"My dad named me."

"Yes, yes. I wanted to," Camile's sigh cut through the air. "I don't know how else to say this, but I must be blunt in this instance."

I had the impression she was always blunt, but I nodded and kept an encouraging smile on my face.

"I must ask you to stay away from Lord Elion," she said.

My fake smile fell. "I don't believe I've met Lord Elion."

"He . . . had a mishap outside on the stairs."

Ah. *Lord* Elion?

"He has a harsh demeanor, and you'd be wise to avoid him," Camile said.

"Do you mean because of his scars? Something like that doesn't bother me."

"His scars bear witness to what he has done," she snapped. Her face loosened, the creases of anger smoothing, but her light gray eyes remained steely.

"What *has* he done?" Why was I pushing this? I should let it go.

Still, I could picture the despair—and hope—in his eyes.

"That is none of your business, human. Stay away from him," she growled. "He is not among the eligible matches, and you will avoid him at all costs."

"Is he married or something?" I had to ask.

"Of course not. Who would have him?"

I didn't answer.

"His curse will continue to twist him until it claims him within one year's time," she said.

"What do you mean by claims him?"

"The curse will drive him out of his mind."

My mouth went dry. He'd seemed okay, but we'd barely talked. A flash of sympathy shot through me.

"All right," I said. "I'll avoid him." It wasn't like I'd ever see him again.

I hurried toward the young fae woman waiting in the foyer.

"See that you do," Camile said as I passed through the archway. "If you're caught in his curse, you will also die."

Chapter 9
Elion

"Please tell Follen to have a bath drawn in my rooms and arrange for formal clothing," I said to one of the castle staff as I strode up the front staircase.

The elf bowed. "Would you like a light meal sent to your rooms as well, sir?"

"Yes, of course." Reaching the landing, I continued to the second floor, limping because I'd banged the wound on my leg when I fell on the stairs.

With a titter, the human females entered the lobby below.

Despite my determination to continue to my rooms and ignore them, I stopped on the third-floor landing and listened.

Because I couldn't see, I moved closer to the railing and peered down.

Raven shone like a jewel among the others, though I couldn't determine why. She was no more attractive than them.

It irritated me that I couldn't ignore her.

I was behaving like a creeper—I believed that was the term humans used for those who stalked others. While I hated succumbing to this need to see her, to be near her, I couldn't seem to hold myself back.

She *was* beautiful in her own way, from her rich brown hair, which should be considered dull. It shone in the low light like the rarest vesarian wood. I'd already noted her dark green eyes, so unusual in the fae world. Perhaps they were common among humans. I hadn't met many.

As if she sensed me watching, she glanced upward.

I slunk back. It wouldn't do for her to see me watching. Keeping her at arm's length was best for everyone. I wouldn't want to cause her pain, and nothing would come from me but that.

I needed to remember she was totally forbidden. Even if I wanted to, I could not make her mine. I'd cruelly told her I would not seek a bride, but a small part of me—that stupid part of my soul I hadn't been able to crush since I was cursed—ached to court and claim her.

Their voices echoed in the foyer, and I watched as Camile Du'patrice strode sedately down to join them. Her calm exterior was a façade. She was as upset about the humans intermarrying with the fae as half the kingdom. It was anyone's guess how this would turn out. If the human women were lucky, they'd find matches who'd treat them kindly.

If they were unlucky . . . I didn't want to think about

that. There wasn't anything I could do, even if I wanted to.

I could only hope they'd remain unobtrusive. If they poked their noses into things they shouldn't, I feared some might wind up dead. Too many of my fellow fae were angry about mixing their blood with ours, though the odds of that were slim. Our species was dying out. Only a few young were born each year.

And that was why we'd sought these matches. Many believed these females would be more fertile than the fae. If so, they could save our race.

Or begin the dilution. The prince's term, not mine. He was one of those opposed to these mergers, something the king sought.

I watched as Camile led the females into the front parlor, my gaze still hawklike on Raven.

She glanced in my direction, and I slunk closer to the wall, letting the shadows hide me from view.

Once they'd left the foyer, I pivoted and continued up two more floors to the suite I used the rare nights I stayed within the castle. Most of my time was spent at my own estate, a dark tomb of a building that was coated in ice more times than not. It hadn't always been that way. My bones remembered a time of sunshine and warmth. Something that was stolen from me when the witch laid her curse.

"Your bath water is ready," Follen said as I entered the room. He swept his arm to the bed where a formal tunic and pants lay on the deep blue bedspread.

"Thank you," I said.

"The kitchen prepared a light repast," Follen said, nodding to the tray sitting on a table near the enormous tub full of steaming water. "I asked them to include a flask of brudeen."

A harsh but heady liquor.

"I appreciate it," I said, truly meaning it. This man was one of the few who didn't scorn me.

He poured a snifter and set the crystal glass close to the tub before bowing. "Will that be all, sir?"

"Yes, thank you. I'll see you in the morning."

"Very well, sir." He strode into the adjoining room and continued through the others. He'd exit in the back hall and take the staff staircase to the lower levels.

I stripped and sunk into the bath, wincing when the water hit my cuts, but groaning with pleasure as I leaned back against the thick wooden tub. The water lapped against my upper chest, and the light fragrance Follen had thought to include sunk into my senses, lulling me.

It didn't take long to wash away the grime and blood from the fight, but I soaked longer, savoring the warmth sinking through my flesh, the meal, and the brudeen relaxing my bones.

When the water cooled, I climbed out and dried quickly, dressing in the clean clothing. I didn't look in the mirror. I *never* looked in mirrors, not since she cursed me with my scarred form. I knew I appeared hideous to the world around me, that I was a terrifying thing to behold. There was no need to reinforce it.

I sat on the edge of the bed to put on my shoes. Follen had buffed them, though the gesture was hardly necessary.

I intended to hang back and observe the festivities, but I would do all I could to avoid catching attention.

And as much as I wanted to, I wouldn't seek Raven.

Leaving my rooms, I took the stairs quickly, drawn to the tinkle of laughter and the clink of fine crystal. The low murmur suggested one hundred, maybe two hundred mingled in the small ballroom on the first floor. It made sense to keep the initial introductions informal. The last thing some wanted to do was to frighten the humans away. The king would've given this directive.

I stood in the doorway, trying to see this through the humans' eyes. Chandeliers dangling from the vaulted ceiling. Gleaming walls and marble floor. Elf staff bustling around the room with trays loaded with drinks.

The king watching it all benignly from his imposing throne sitting on the dais on the left side of the room.

My gaze sought Raven, and I didn't question why. Perhaps I was merely curious. Like most of the fae, I had only met a few humans. They were intriguing.

It was nothing else.

Dressed in a simple yet elegant afternoon gown of rich green I believe matched her eyes, she stood with one of the other women, laughing at something one lord said. Other males clustered around, seeking her, just like I was.

No. I did not seek her. I needed to remind myself of that.

Her smile fell, and a small frown knit her brow.

When her gaze sought mine, I froze, unsure what to do. I was not welcome here. I needed to leave.

Swallowing deeply, I strode toward her.

Chapter 10
Raven

Shit. Lord Elion was walking toward me.

Maybe me. I glanced over my shoulder because he could be striding toward someone else. It wouldn't be the first time I got gushy over a guy I thought was coming my way, only to feel my face flame as he strode past me and up to someone more exciting than me.

No one was looking his way, but still.

My spine tightened, and I shot the fae guys chatting with me and Betts a bright smile. Great cover.

I felt Elion stop beside me.

Okay, so maybe he wanted to speak with the fae guys. Or . . . Betts. I didn't look his way. I *couldn't* look his way. The last time we talked, he pretty much blew me off, and that still stung. I'd be open to him groveling, however.

Both of the fae guys bowed to Elion.

"Lord Elion," Lord Nuvian said. "I didn't think you were attending the events."

"Neither did I," Elion said in a voice that made my

knees loosen. So far, none of the fae guys had sparked my interest. Sure, they were all gorgeous, and I had to admit, the flattery and kissing up made me feel heady, but after twenty minutes into this event and meeting six or eight fae lords, my resolve to return home had not wavered.

"Do you need something, sir?" Nuvian asked.

"No."

The weight of Elion's gaze fell on me, and I wasn't sure what I should do. The polite thing would be to turn and smile.

"Allow me to introduce Lord Elion Daeven Luthaistras Iliric Fendove," Nuvian said.

"Whoa," Betts breathed. She leaned close to me. "Try saying that one fast." She eased around me and extended her hand. "Nice to meet you, Lord Elion. I'm Bettina Anna Blake. Betts for short."

Elion took her hand and bowed before releasing it. "Delighted."

"And this is Raven Wilder," Nuvian said, nodding to me.

"Kathryn," I interjected.

"Excuse me?" Nuvian asked.

Aillun, the other fae guy Betts and I had been chatting with, watched us through black, hawklike eyes. His intent gaze went from Elion to me, but as far as I knew, there wasn't anything exciting to see here. Just five people talking.

"Kathryn is my middle name," I said. I wasn't sure if I should offer to shake Elion's hand or not. I didn't need to set myself up for a second rejection.

He moved to stand beside Nuvian, facing me, and lifted his hand my way, his palm up. "A pleasure."

Was it? The jury was still out on that. Sure, I couldn't stop thinking about him, but that didn't mean I could ignore how he'd behaved. However, by the blood on his face and the tears in his clothing, he'd tussled with something vicious. He'd fallen to his knees in front of us, which would be embarrassing enough for me to hide in my room for days.

I could cut him some slack. Maybe he'd been cranky about what caused his wounds, and it had nothing to do with me.

I placed my hand in his, struggling to keep my face neutral when my fingers essentially tingled. I didn't like that I couldn't control my body's response to him. So far, I could easily dismiss all the fae guys vying for my hand in marriage.

Elion? He was a whole different ball game.

He bowed low over my hand, and his lips brushed the back of my fingers. Heat shot through me, centering between my legs, and I bit back my gasp.

This guy was deadly. If he turned on the charm, I'd topple like a tree in a stiff wind.

He straightened, and the smile teasing across his lips suggested he could read my thoughts. I hadn't heard the fae were mind readers, but nothing would surprise me.

However, they *could* use magic to lull someone, and that could be what I was feeling. They assured us the fae wouldn't use their magic on us, but I'd lived long enough to know people might agree to one thing but do whatever they wanted after that.

I tugged my fingers away from his.

"Would you like to go out onto the balcony?" he asked, waving toward the tall open doors. I'd peeked out there earlier, admiring the gorgeous gardens and carved stone pillars supporting the weight of the deck above.

Nuvian and Aillun's dark eyebrows lifted, but they said nothing.

"Sure," I mean, why not? I could guard my heart from this man.

He held out his arm, and I placed my fingers on it, noting the twitch of his muscles beneath the rich sleeve of his formal tunic.

Earlier, the staff had primped me as if I was going to a cartoon Disney ball, and at the time, I'd grumbled. How in the world was I supposed to walk in a puffy, long skirt? And my nipples kept threatening to peek above the low-cut bodice.

After helping me dress, a second set of elves descended to fix my hair. They'd twisted it up into an elaborate arrangement with strategic curls draping down to tease my bare neck and shoulders. All I needed was a crown, and I could call myself a princess.

As we walked across the room, weaving around clusters of fae and humans, the satin dress felt amazing gliding across my lower legs. I lifted my chin, feeling as if I fit in here, something that hadn't happened while growing up. Mom did her best, but we hadn't had much.

I was grateful I hadn't balked when the staff showed up to help me get ready. I liked looking my best for Elion.

Silly girl, I chided myself. He wasn't interested; he was only being polite. For all I knew, he'd blow me off again once we were outside.

We'd almost made it to the open double doors when a shriek rang out to my right.

Camile stormed over to stand between us and the door, her arms spread wide. "I warned you, Raven." Her hands lifted, and she shot a bolt of something electrical at me.

My body stiffened.

I couldn't move even if I wanted to.

In fact, I couldn't speak.

Or breathe.

Chapter 11
Elion

When Camile cast an immobile spell on Raven, fury consumed me. I would rip her apart. I stomped between her and Raven, who remained motionless. Her panic-stricken gaze had frozen in a forward position, and I could almost hear the scream locked in her throat.

But before I could slam Camile with a spell that would incinerate her on the spot, the king rose from his throne.

"Camile!" He hurried down the dais and across the room, a fleet of guards accompanying him.

A snarl erupted from his throat, and with a wave of his hand, Camile's spell dissipated, leaving only the faint smell of rotten eggs in the air.

Raven gulped in air, and when she staggered, I tugged her against me, wishing more than anything that I could wrap my arms around her. No, I wanted to lift her into my arms and storm from this room, taking her some place where no one would ever harm her.

But things could get nasty if I showed interest in this female.

"How dare you?" the king snarled at Camile. "These humans are our guests." His anger, a living wall of black mist, impacted with Camile, and she stumbled away from him, her arms lifting as she hit the wall near the opening to the balcony.

Her gaze swept the room before she sneered at the king. "*You* are responsible for this, and you will pay." A pop, and she disappeared.

"Go after her," the king growled. "*I* will deal with her."

In other words, not me.

Three guards gave chase, disappearing to pursue her in the inner realm. Hopefully, her slight lead didn't give her the chance to get away.

The inner realm was a dark place full of corridors and screams. It was unwise to travel there for long or you'd find yourself trapped within the realm's sinister embrace. Camile would use one of the many passages to escape into another part of the kingdom.

However, the king's guards were master wizards and extremely loyal to the royal family. If anyone could follow and capture Camile, it would be them. They'd bring her back, and she'd suffer for daring to harm a guest.

Things were tenuous enough in the kingdom already.

Many opposed bringing the human brides here, and some weren't above ensuring the potential matches failed.

If Camile got away with this, others would feel empowered to do the same.

The king turned to Raven and slanted his head. His deep blue eyes shadowed with dismay, and when he bowed, his black hair shot through with silver gleamed in the low lights. "I apologize. I will ensure she is punished. I also promise you that something like this will never happen again." He pressed his fist against his chest. "This, I vow."

And this was why this older fae male was revered by the kingdom. His ancestors may have killed each other more often than not, and his father might've been responsible for the deadly purge thirty years ago, one that resulted in half the aristocracy being wiped out with one magical blow, but King Khaidill had integrity. Honor.

I'd give my life to save his.

Raven stepped away from me, though she shot me a look of thanks. "I'm sure she didn't mean . . . harm."

Diplomacy at its best.

"You are too kind," King Khaidill said. His gaze drifted to the balcony, and he sighed. His personal attendants flanked him, their attention constantly surveying the gathering crowd. Picking up the distressed murmurs from the other humans and many in attendance, he pressed for a smile. "As an apology, I would like to present you with a small gift."

"Oh, you don't need to do anything like that," Raven said, her pretty cheeks pinkening.

"I would like to."

No one denied the king when his voice thickened with resolve, and Raven responded like any other.

"Thank you, then. That's sweet of you," she said, her gaze dropping from Khaidill's. It rose to meet mine, and more color filled her face.

I could watch out for her, my gaze feasting on her lush form, her rich brown hair, and her unusual, teal-colored eyes. My longing for this woman was a pervasive ache in my chest. I could try to fight it, but in my soul, I knew these feelings would not be denied.

If I was wise, I'd leave the palace this instant and travel to my icy estate. I'd remain there until she'd wed another.

"Would a gift like this turn your questionable afternoon into something exciting?" the king said. He loved to give unusual presents. Raven couldn't be aware of the honor that comes with receiving any attention from the king.

A flick of his hand, and a long-haired resha kit appeared by her feet. Nearly extinct, the fluffy creature wasn't much bigger than my fist, though it would grow larger. They were revered as pets, though only the most elite could apply to adopt them.

As far as I knew, only five adults existed within the kingdom. Leave it to King Khaidill to gift Raven with one of the coveted offspring from his own mating pair. I'd heard four kits were born a few months ago.

"Oh, my," Raven said, stooping down to stroke the creature's head. Its bushy, spiked tail whipped back and forth, and it sniffed her fingers. Resha's bonded with only one being in their lifetime. Would the kit accept or reject this human?

Its fur rippled, and its shiny coat changed from deep brown to the brightest gold.

Raven's breath caught, and she shot widened eyes toward the king. "What happened?"

"He has chosen you," the king said with a low laugh. "Why does this not surprise me?" His gaze met mine, and I sensed something more in his statement.

"So sweet." Raven smiled up at the king, her face full of wonder. "Thank you."

Other than its spiked tail and long, vicious claws, a full-grown resha would grow a bit larger than what humans called house cats. Exceedingly loyal, they'd been known to save their bonded being's lives. A fitting, though unusual, gift for Raven.

"Can I pick it up?" she asked.

"Of course you can. He is yours." The king chuckled, and those around him echoed the sound, though a few barked shrilly.

I hadn't realized until this second that they'd remained silent, listening and taking their cue from how he treated the situation. Camile was respected throughout the kingdom. I was surprised by her behavior. It was considered an honor to host the newcomers.

However, this would show those who hoped to interfere with the brides that any attempt to thwart the process would be met with harsh discipline. And that the humans were considered equal to those of the highest ranks in the kingdom.

Raven straightened with the resha in her arms, shooting a smile my way as she nuzzled the tiny beast's golden fur.

The king lifted his hand. "I believe we need to return to the festivities."

Murmurs of agreement erupted around him. The crowd thinned as the guests returned to the conversation they'd been engaged in before Camile's insurrection.

"Enjoy the kit," the king told Raven. "We'll speak later?"

"Of course," she said. "Thank you again."

"I'll have one of my staff place the resha within your rooms," he said. His attention shot to me before returning to her. "Then you can enjoy the afternoon and evening."

"That would be great," Raven said, handing the resha over to one of the king's own personal entourage. The stately elf would take the resha to Raven's room and guard it with her life.

The king left us, and his guards went with him, striding back to his throne and sitting. His arms lifted. "Music. We need music!"

A perfect way to lighten the mood. In the corner, a nymph quartet lifted their handcrafted instruments, and a light, flowery tune drifted through the room.

"Are you all right?" I asked Raven, still churning inside about what Camile had done.

"I am, thanks." She nodded to the balcony. "We were going outside, weren't we?"

I was pleased that she could put this behind her. Hopefully, it would be her only unpleasant experience in the kingdom.

She took my arm again, and I led her outside.

The sun lingered on the horizon, stabbing gold and deep red beams through the forest and up into the sky.

"It's beautiful here," Raven said, leaning against a stone railing. "I still can't believe it's all happening."

"I hope things will go as they should for you from now on." A neutral statement, but despite my need to be near her, my tongue felt as frozen as if Camile had cast a spell on it too.

There were so many things I wanted to say to Raven, but I couldn't seem to find the words.

Raven's arm swept out. "Look at the gardens. And the fountains. It's gorgeous."

As if on cue, water shot into the sky, sparkling in the burnished sunset like the rarest of strings of blood-red jewels.

Her breath caught, and she leaned over the railing, squinting toward the largest fountain in the center of the back garden. "What's . . .?" A shudder ripped through her, and she backed away, her arm lifting. "There's something . . . No, there's *someone* in the water."

What? I leaned over the rail.

A female dressed in the kingdom's finest, a gown I'd noted one of the human women wearing, floated face down in the water.

I raced to the end of the deck and leaped down the

stairs, running over to the fountain. After pulling her from the water, I laid her carefully on the ground.

Raven joined me, standing on the woman's other side, her hands fretting at her neck. "It's Crystal. Crystal Hurst! She's . . . We've got to do something for her."

From the lack of color in her face, she'd been dead at least twenty minutes.

A high-pitched cackle echoed in the woods.

"Get help," I barked, rising. I scanned the woods, catching movement deep within the brush.

While Raven hurried up the stairs and inside, I turned and bolted toward the forest.

I hit the tree line at a dead run, sticks and brush whipping my body.

The woods closed around me, locking me within its deadly embrace, and my steps slowed. When I spun to return to the castle, I smacked into an invisible wall.

Raven stood on the other side, her wide eyes meeting mine.

A mist-like creature glided up behind her, its snake-like limbs reaching for her neck.

Chapter 12
Raven

Red marks encircled Crystal's neck, like something had latched on, and held tight until she stopped struggling. Her hair had come down from its pretty arrangement and resembled dead seaweed washed up on the shore. She wasn't moving or breathing.

"Get help," Elion said, and that unlocked my legs. I ran up the stairs, across the balcony, and stumbled into the big ballroom where we'd gathered for the afternoon soiree. Somehow, during all the "fun," night had fallen.

"She's . . . She's . . ." I sputtered to no one in particular, my wild gaze taking in the surreal setting. How could anyone laugh when Crystal had been murdered?

They universally ignored me, chatting with each other or bellying up to the long table across the room with light snacks we'd been told to barely touch—by Camile. The women who'd warned me away from Elion. Who'd tried to steal the breath from my lungs.

Had she killed Crystal instead of taking her fury out on me?

My heart slammed around in my chest, and my breathing whistled along my throat. Dizzy, I worried I'd pass out. Her dusky face and limp body kept flashing through my mind.

I hated feeling guilty, but it could've been me. Camile had threatened to get even.

I shook my head and rushed through the room, approaching the throne where the king sat chatting with a cluster of retainers. When I got within ten feet of him, two guards disappeared from beside him and reappeared in front of me, their arms outstretched to block access to the king. Did they think I'd attack him?

Hysterical laughter bubbled through me. Nope, I wasn't going to kill the king, but it appeared someone had killed one of us.

"I need to talk to the king," I said, my voice tight with horror.

"Release her," King Khaidill said with a benevolent sweep of his hand.

The guards backed away, and I approached the throne. I stopped in front of him and curtsied, unsure if this was the right way to greet the fae king, but assumed there was no harm in showing deference.

He nodded, encouraging me to speak.

"Crystal is dead," I whispered.

He frowned and glanced at the retainer standing closest to him. "Excuse me?"

"I said Crystal is dead!"

Of course, at that very moment, the musicians had paused between songs. Conversation had naturally stilled, and my voice echoed in the big room like a bullhorn.

Someone shrieked. "Crystal?"

Others rushed toward me. I gulped and backed away, hurrying toward the balcony. "Crystal is dead. She . . . Lord Elion and I found her floating face down in the fountain."

They followed me outside and down the stairs, their hoarse cries making my pulse flail in my throat.

When I reached Crystal lying on the ground, I continued past her, leaving them to address the situation.

I had to find out what happened to Elion. He'd run into the woods, and I worried whoever hurt Crystal would do the same to him.

When I reached the dark forest, my footsteps slowed, but I didn't stop. I entered along the trail I'd seen Elion take, my footsteps light as I peered around, seeking him.

I'd heard the cackle after we pulled Crystal from the fountain. Was it the murderer?

That was assuming Crystal hadn't drowned, though I had no idea why she'd climb into the fountain and somehow drown in a pool that was only a few feet deep, let alone gain strangulation marks on her throat.

No, someone had killed her.

"Elion?" I whispered, feeling stupid for wandering around in the dark. Someone just hurt Crystal. Camile had threatened me. And now I was stumbling around the woods in the dark.

I should turn around and return to the others where it was safer, though Crystal sure hadn't been safe back there.

I spied movement farther inside the woods.

Stopping on the path, I squinted. Moonlight outlined Elion ahead.

Okay, I'd join him. He'd watch out for me. I hoped. No, he would. He might've sneered on the steps, but he'd been polite after that.

I rushed forward and slammed into something clear and solid. Backing up a few steps, I rubbed my shoulder where it took the impact.

"What's going on?" I asked Elion, fear climbing my spine.

His gaze traveled past me, and my skin prickled. Something was behind me . . .

This was why people shouldn't wander in the woods at night. They could wind up like Crystal.

Turning, I gulped. Dark had coalesced into something unimaginable. It resembled a demon from picture books. No, a hyena the size of a pony. It crept toward me, shifting and morphing, turning from one terrifying creature into another while I stood frozen.

Run!

I spun and bolted, my hands lifted, and smacked into the invisible barrier again. My panic-stricken gaze met Elion's. I shrieked, trying to claw my way through, but it felt impervious to even a nuclear explosion.

Fear boiled inside me. The mist creature would grab me while Elion watched.

I'd started to turn—to face the death I was convinced this creature would deliver—when Elion's face twisted. He hunched forward, his arms dangling in the air. A shudder ripped through his body, and silvery-gray fur took the place of his clothing.

He landed on the path on four padded feet, his silver fur gleaming and his glowing eyes turned my way.

Wait . . . This was the wolf I'd seen back home, but it couldn't be.

Elion was a wolf shifter. A thing like that shouldn't exist outside of novels, yet—

He leaped, slamming into the clear barrier. Again.

A scream erupted around us and I felt, rather than saw, the barrier drop.

Snarling, Elion jumped onto the mist creature, and they fell to the ground in a tangle of slashing limbs.

Chapter 13
Elion

If I didn't eliminate this threat, it would go after Raven.

Nothing would pain me more. I shouldn't be drawn to her. If I was a decent person, I'd walk away.

I just couldn't make myself do it.

Since I couldn't do magic in my wolf form, I shifted into my normal form.

The mist creature rushed toward me, morphing into a boar, slashing its tusks. I reeled my head back, and the tusks dragged across my throat. An inch closer, and it would've ripped out my windpipe.

I kicked, dislodging the boar, and it scrambled for purchase on the rotted leaves. A musky-sour smell filled the air, partly from the leaves but also from the creature.

Leaping to my feet, I gathered magic and shot it at the boar. It shuddered and shifted, flashing from a tiny frog to the boar, and then to a dragon. Arching its neck, it reared up over me, growing stronger and bigger as it sucked in power.

It blasted fire, and I leaped to the side.

"Run," I bellowed at Raven while the world ignited around us. She stood frozen, watching with her jaw unhinged.

My cry must've reminded her very little stood between the dragon and her, because she skittered down the trail. I didn't look in her direction after that.

The dragon leaped, knocking me backward and pinning me to the ground before I could wound it with my inner fire. I wrangled with it, struggling to keep it from ripping out my neck with its misty claws. Bucking, I tried to dislodge it.

It was too heavy, and my power too crushed by the curse placed upon me for no good reason.

I smacked the dragon's head, but my hand passed through it.

It pressed me down, its teeth going for my throat . . .

A thick stick smacked through the creature, and with a pop, it exploded, sending misty dust blasting into the air. The foul taint of brimstone and ash lingered.

The stick dropped to the ground with a thud, followed by Raven landing on her knees beside me.

She grabbed my shoulder. "Are you alive? Please tell me you're alive!"

Overcome with adrenaline and amazed by her actions, I latched onto her arms and rolled until I'd pinned her beneath me.

"Oh, my," she breathed, blinking up at me. "I'd say you're alive."

I'd show her I lived.

Lowering my head, I claimed her mouth with my own.

She moaned, and her arms glided around my shoulders. While I delved into her mouth with my tongue, she fisted my hair, holding tight.

Our tongues twisted together, and heat spiraled within me, a flame I feared even fate couldn't extinguish.

She rocked her hips up against me, and it was all I could do not to strip her and give her what she craved.

My hand slid up her thigh, but when I touched between her legs, she gasped and jerked her head away from mine.

"Elion," she said, and I was grateful not to hear horror or disgust in her voice. "I think . . . Hell, I'm not sure I can form a single thought after that kiss."

I grinned. I couldn't help it.

I levered myself up and off her, taking her hand to tug her off the ground. I ached to wrap my arms around her. Ached to kiss her again.

That wouldn't do. It was forbidden.

Hell, *I* was forbidden. Being near her endangered her life.

And let us not forget my expected and untimely death due a year from now.

Cursed, I would soon die.

I'd be a fool to take her on this ride, despite how delectable she'd felt beneath me.

"Go to the castle, little human," I said gruffly, my voice overcome with emotion. What was it about this female? I should back away from her.

Run from her.

"Little human, huh?" Her lips quirked up on one side. "I'm not so little, though I guess I'm human."

I lifted one eyebrow. "Do you doubt who you come from?"

She shrugged. "Dad ditched me and Mom when I was little. I never knew him. As for my mom," she gulped, "she died a short time ago." Her gaze fell, and she swallowed. Sorrow swirled around her, thick and full of pain.

If only I could hold her. Comfort her. Take her to my estate where I could make sure no one and nothing ever hurt her.

I growled, and she darted a look up at me.

"You're offended that my father bailed on me and my mother?" she asked, the bite in her voice sinking through my skin.

"He was foolish not to stay with you."

"He doesn't deserve one second of my time." Bitterness tainted her words. "I'm better off without him."

"I understand."

She huffed. "How could you?"

"My own father was . . ." I sighed, aching to share while at the same time, knowing I needed to send her away and never seek her company again.

"A wolf shifter?"

"That, I got all on my own." It was all I could do not to gnash my teeth. "It's a curse."

ICE LORD'S BRIDE

She shrugged. "Might be cool. You know. Running through the woods. Howling at the moon." The sparkle in her eyes invited me to laugh along with her.

That would never do. "It is not cool!"

"So tell me, then. What about your father . . .?" She waited patiently, and I could tell she actually wanted to hear what I had to say.

I'd kissed her. I would do anything to possess her.

But joining with me could drag her into the curse and kill her.

"I said you need to go," I snarled, angry with myself for speaking with her. I should've avoided the reception.

I should've avoided her.

Her growl rang out, and her cheeks pinkened with fury. I'd never seen a more beautiful woman. "Don't share if you don't want to, then." She stomped her foot. "I get it. You're a prince—"

"*Lord.*"

"Whatever." Storming past me, she headed toward the castle.

Turning, I watched her flee.

If only I could watch her forever.

Chapter 14
Raven

I ran down the trail, aiming for the lights shining from the castle ahead.

When I bumped into someone on the path, I shrieked.

Behind me, a growl ripped through the air.

I struggled to break free of a relentless grip, finally wrenching myself away. Stumbling backward, I impacted with someone else. I cried out, whirling, only to release a heavy breath when I found Elion in wolf form standing on the trail, his paws clawing at the musty leaves and his fur standing on end.

He shifted back to fae form and moved around me.

"She was with me," he told the other guy. The air shimmered, and his face smoothed into . . . I now identified him as one of the fae who'd come to the diner before I was chosen for what was beginning to feel like a deadly farce. Lord Nuvian had been in the diner? This meant . . .

Wait. The fae guy I'd gotten the hots for, the one who'd almost appeared glamoured—

"It was you in the diner," I said, glaring at Elion. I didn't understand why the idea made me mad, but it did. Actually, I was mad that I'd put myself in a position where he could reject me again.

Elion dipped his head forward.

"You need to leave," Lord Nuvian said, and I wasn't sure if he was speaking to me or Elion.

"Nuvian is my advisor," Elion said, his hand flicking forward.

"I'm Raven, but we've already met." My lips were a thin slash on my face. I dared him with my eyes to tell me everything.

He stared at my outstretched hand until Elion growled again.

"A pleasure to meet you again," Nuvian said, taking my hand briefly before releasing it. His attention shot to Elion. "Why did you leave without informing us of where you were going?"

"I'm not a child in need of supervision," Elion said, shouldering past Nuvian. He turned and huffed at me. "And I told you to get back to the castle."

I crossed my arms over my chest and tapped my foot on the ground. "If I want to wander around in the woods at night, I will. I do not need your permission." I had no intention of coming to the woods again, not after what I'd seen, but he didn't need to know that.

Nuvian stepped back and watched us, amusement teasing across his lips.

Fury churned inside me. I refused to be mocked by these guys. I'd come here for the chance to better my life. To pretend I'd consider marriage, then say no way and collect my consolation prize. There was nothing wrong with that.

I didn't need their respect or for them to like me.

Storming past them, I stomped out of the woods and across the lawn, joining those milling around the fountain. Crystal's body was gone.

"Where have you been?" Betts asked, rushing to my side and pumping my arm. "I didn't see you anywhere, and I was worried." Her gaze shot to the fountain. "This is horrible. No one seems to know what happened, but they're saying she drank a little too much and went into the water and drowned."

"She had strangulation marks on her neck."

Betts's fingers went to her lips, fluttering. "Oh, no, she didn't. I looked specifically. She drowned. It was an accident."

I'd seen the marks, hadn't I?

Out of the corner of my eye, I saw Elion and Nuvian leaving the woods. They skirted along the edge that necklaced the back of the castle and were soon gone from view.

Not gone from my mind, however. Elion, that is. I couldn't care less about his "advisor," Nuvian, who'd acted like I had scabies when I offered him my hand for a shake.

"We should all return inside," King Khaidill said, a

slight shake coming through in his voice. His gaze kept drifting to the woods.

There was something going on here. While it was clear some of the fae didn't approve of us being here, were they upset about it enough to kill?

"I don't believe the festivities should continue today, however," the king added, moving past us with his entourage surrounding him. His gaze shot to me and Betts. "Please, I invite all of you to join me in the main dining room for the morning meal. We will have a moment of silence to remember our poor friend Crystal."

And then what? We get back to the fae dating game? I didn't like this, not one bit, but what could I do? I was essentially trapped here until the program had run its course.

We followed the others into the castle.

"Please welcome your new advisor, Axilya," the king said once we stood in the back foyer. He gestured to a tall fae woman lurking in the shadows near a doorway leading to a hall.

The tall woman stepped forward into the light, revealing her milk-white hair streaked through with sparkles, a perfect example of what many humans, plus my cousin, hoped to emulate. Her long, pale blue robe brushed across her silver shoes as she bowed to the king. "I would be delighted to assume this responsibility, your highness."

"Very well," he said while me and the other three women essentially clung together in the small, though equally gilded, entrance. He strode past us and into the hall, his entourage fluttering along behind him. This left us alone with Axilya.

"Come, come," Axilya said, clapping her hands. "A death is a distressing event, but we must not let it sway us from our purpose."

"Cold-blooded, isn't she?" Betts said, her voice low.

Axilya frowned, deepening the creases already present in her older face. I'd heard the fae lived a very long time. How old was Axilya?

"I suggest you return to your rooms and remain there for the rest of the day. Please join me in the lobby tomorrow, ten minutes before nine. Your detail will ensure you are ready. I suggest you do as they ask and avoid interfering with the process."

And what did that mean? Had Crystal "interfered?"

A chill shot through me, and I had the sense that everything was changing.

Change? Ha. Things had changed the moment the fae showed up in our world. Would this change be for the better or make things worse?

"I'll go with you," Betts said. "My room is in the same wing as yours."

I nodded, and we walked through the castle to the front lobby. Guards left positions along the wall to escort us—or make sure we went inside and remained there.

They wouldn't want anyone else stepping into the fountain for a swim, now would they?

Betts and I split outside my room, and a guard took a position near the wall opposite my door.

"See you in the morning," Betts said, spontaneously

hugging me. She placed her lips near my ear. "Watch out," she whispered. "Be careful what you say."

Huh. Maybe she *had* seen marks on Crystal's neck. If so, that meant my assumption was correct. Someone murdered her. Others removed the marks to confuse us. These were the fae; they could do magic on a whim.

Camile was my primary suspect, of course, but she was only one of those who'd scowled at us during the reception.

Some might want us here, but many didn't. We'd have to be careful with the latter.

"Good night," I said softly. "Watch your back."

Stepping away from me, she nodded. Tears made her fear-filled eyes shimmer, and my own stung. I hadn't known Crystal, but she was one of us, not them. I didn't like feeling as if we were two feuding factions, but if there was a murderer among us, we might need to take that approach.

I went inside while she continued down the hall with her escort.

With a sigh, I leaned against the door.

"My name is Maecia. I'll help you undress?" an elf woman asked, coming out of the bathing chamber attached to my room. Her hands fretted at her sides, and her long, pale pink gown swayed around her. She'd flattened her silver wings against her back.

"I can undress alone, but thanks," I said, noting the nightgown she must've laid on the bed.

"Would you like me to fetch a repast for you from the kitchens, then? A sweet or a full meal?"

"No, thanks." I pressed for a smile. "I'm all set for the night. Truly."

She bowed. "Very well. I'll wake you promptly at eight, then, to help you rise and prepare for the morning event."

Did everyone here need help rising and preparing? It sure seemed so.

"All right." My lips thinned. I dreaded what might be coming. Was the king going to take five minutes to reflect on Crystal's loss, then pretend nothing happened? It sure looked like it. Crystal's life mattered.

And her death sure as hell hadn't come from drowning.

The elf left and, restless, I strode around my room, crossing back and forth before undressing and putting on a nightie that draped to my knees. With a huff, I slumped on the firm blue cushion spanning the window seat.

Movement below on the back of the lawn and near the woods drew my eye.

A wolf stood there, staring toward my window.

Elion.

Rising, I crept to the bathroom window. Escaping through the hall wasn't an option. I lifted the window and stepped out onto the low, sloped roof. Three stories up was too big a jump, but the roof in this section sloped down to a garden where I'd seen a series of trellises earlier. Were they sturdy enough to support my weight?

I was about to find out.

Chapter 15
Elion

Why was I lurking in the back garden? I stomped my front paw on the dew-covered grass. And because I felt like a stupid, lovesick fool watching her window from the back lawn in wolf form, I shifted back to my fae body.

And paced some more.

"Fountain guard duty?" Raven asked in a voice lilting with humor. She skipped across the lawn toward me, dressed only in a nightgown, her feet bare. The moonlight behind her outlined her delicious curves.

I craved . . .

My cock responded to the sight, beginning to stiffen.

"You shouldn't be here," I snarled.

She sighed. "Are we back there again? Grumpy, grumpy, grumpy, aren't you?"

I growled, my wolf rising in my throat.

Her spine stiffened, and she lifted one eyebrow. "I'm not afraid of you." Her hair gleamed in the moonlight, and I ached to run my fingers through it, to grab onto it while I kissed her.

"You should be."

"Since we're playing games, I'll say you probably shouldn't be out here either."

"I am in line for the throne, which suggests I have more right to be here than you," I said, feeling like a fool the moment the words passed my lips. This woman scrambled my mind. She made me dream. Both were equally dangerous.

"No need to get snooty with me." She deepened her voice, mocking me. "I'm in line for the throne. You are a lowly human." Sighing, she sat on a stone bench. Tall for a human, her feet still dangled, her toes with bright pink painted tips. They were cute as far as toes went.

Why in all hell was I thinking about her toes?

Perhaps it was better to think about her delicate toes than dream about pressing her against a tree and claiming her.

I was beginning to believe I was hopeless against her charms.

"Stop trying to lure me," I said.

She patted the bench beside her, and like a well-behaved pup, I sat before defying her crossed my mind.

"You know I can't do magic, so even if I wanted to lure you closer, I wouldn't be able to."

I turned to fully face her, unable to look away. She stared forward, her tiny chin lifted and her lips a straight, alluring slash on her face.

"Do you wish to lure me?" I asked.

She flashed a glance my way before facing forward again. "Would it do any good if I said yes?"

"You need to stay away from me."

"You've shoved me away twice now. Yet, here you are, pacing in the back lawn, staring up at my window."

"I was looking at the moon."

"Do you howl?"

I stiffened. "Excuse me?"

She laughed softly and turned my way, hitching her leg up and bending it. Her cute toes dangled off the edge of the bench. "I meant, when you're in wolf form, do you howl at the moon?"

"Why would I do that?"

"Why not?" She shrugged, and her breasts moved beneath the thin fabric. I could almost see the ripe buds of her nipples, and I wanted to slash through the material to expose them. Taste them.

Growling, I raked my fingers through my hair.

"You've got the growl down pat, so why not howl? Let it all out. I sense you're frustrated about something."

"I *am* frustrated," I snapped.

"About what? Your fur isn't glossy enough? You wish your claws were sharper?"

"Nothing like that."

"Then what is it?" A challenge came through in her voice.

I worried this female would soon be able to wrap me around her wrist like a bracelet. She'd wear me for a while, but what would happen when she tired of her trinket?

"I want to kiss you," I gnashed my teeth. "Touch you."

"Then what's stopping you?" Another dare.

Her eyes gleamed, and if I didn't know better, I'd believe lust shone there. But she couldn't be attracted to my scarred form and nasty manner. I'd done all I could to drive her away.

My hands shook when I lifted them, and I prayed she didn't see. But when I touched her face and neck, gliding my knuckles across her smooth skin, I forgot about everything but her.

As I'd ached to do, I traced my fingers beneath her hair. I fisted a bunch of it, holding her steady.

Did I think she'd pull away?

Yes.

When she only stared up at me, and I read true lust in her eyes, I claimed her mouth. I would show her she was playing with someone who'd burn her to a crisp.

But the moment our mouths touched, I was the one claimed, the one singed.

She moaned and rose onto her knees, grabbing my shoulders to pull me closer.

A voracious need rose inside me, and it would not be denied. My fingers released her hair to glide down her back. Reaching her lush ass, I hauled her fully against me.

I traced the seam of her lips, and she opened her mouth, welcoming me inside. A groan wracked through me, and I knew right then that this female was dangerous. I craved her, and I feared I would crave her forever.

Still, I couldn't push her away. I released her ass and while my tongue tangled with hers, I slid my hand up beneath her gown, cupping her breast. The nipple budded for me alone, and I couldn't help myself.

I lowered her onto the bench and rose over her, yanking up her gown.

She moaned and arched her spine as I stroked her breast with my hand.

Nothing could make me pull my mouth from hers, my fingers away from her glorious skin.

When I rolled her nipple, she gasped against my mouth and jerked her hips toward my touch.

I glided my fingers down her belly. She wore nothing beneath her gown, and I saw red. Nothing and no one could stop me from feeling everything she offered.

Her legs parted, and I stroked her tight curls, gliding my thumb down her slit. I dipped it inside her, finding her tight and incredibly wet.

Leaving her mouth, I kissed along her jaw to her neck.

She clutched my shoulders, trying to tug my body down onto hers.

My fingers found her clit, and I rubbed while my thumb delved deeply within her.

She panted, lifting her hips up to meet the thrust of my thumb.

I wanted to rip my clothing away and find my soul within her welcoming body.

I would soon. I couldn't stop this any more than I could halt a tsunami racing toward the shore.

Her body convulsed beneath me; her sharp cries sweeter than warm honey. As she gave into her pleasure, her groan ripped from her throat, raw and pure.

I captured her mouth, captured her cries.

Nothing would stop me from claiming this woman now.

Chapter 16
Raven

The next morning, Maecia woke me and insisted I rise right away. No way. I wanted to lie beneath the covers and remember Elion's touch.

They told me he was forbidden, but I couldn't seem to stay away. He drew me in, and all I could think of was him.

"You will wear this," Maecia said, holding up a gown that looked like it stepped out of the Regency era. Puffy at the shoulders, though form-hugging along the arms. A rounded bodice topped a high waistline tied with a band of silver. The hem would brush the tops of my shoes, if I guessed correctly.

Maecia was incredibly beautiful with her willow-thin form, long silver hair, and her perfectly sculpted features.

I slid out of bed but cringed when she tried to remove my nightgown.

She clicked her tongue. "Your bath awaits. Why do

you hesitate? We must get you ready quickly." She clapped her hands for emphasis.

Near the window, a big tub filled with steaming water appeared.

"Please," she said, tugging on the hem of my nightie. "Remove this and get in the water. No shrinking away. I've seen it all, and I don't care what you look like."

In many ways, her matter-of-fact behavior was welcome. It was nice not to hear scorn in her voice. I'd heard many of the fae didn't want us here, but so far, Maecia didn't appear to be among them. But then, they wouldn't assign her to me if that was the case.

When in Rome . . .

I let her help me out of my nightie, which disappeared the second it left my body, perhaps being magicked to the laundry room somewhere in the bowels of the castle.

I made quick work of bathing, then lounged, my head resting on the side of the tub, my eyes closed. Until something brushed against my hair.

Yelping, I sat upright. Water sloshed around, nearly cresting the sides of the tub. I reeled around to find the resha perched on the bath surround.

Its bright gold fluffy coat gleamed in the sunlight, and it flicked its bushy, spiked tail. When my eyes met its silver ones, it released a rumbling purr. Had this creature truly chosen me? That's what the king said.

I held out my finger, and it sniffed before licking the digit, its scratchy tongue tickling.

"You are so cute," I said, and the rumble in its chest

grew louder. "I guess you need a name, don't you? Are you a boy or girl? Because that'll make a difference."

"It is a boy," Maecia called from across the room, where she fussed with the clothing I'd ditched last night. I'd forgotten she was there.

"So, a boy's name then," I said. "Hmm. How about Moonbeam?" I swore he frowned. "Peridot?" His frown deepened. "How about Koko, then?"

He bared his tiny fangs.

"Koko it is," I said.

"You need to get out, please," Maecia said kindly. "I've only seen a resha once in my life. It's a true honor for the king to gift you with a kit." She studied my face like she expected to see a symbol blazing on my forehead that would prove I was worthy. "They only bond with one person in their lifetime."

"Huh."

Koko hopped off the tub and skittered across the room, leaping up onto the bed. He circled about a billion times before settling in the middle, his bushy tail coiled around his body and covering his pointy, fox-like nose.

"How do I take care of him?" I asked, my heart a lump of mush for him already.

"You don't. His handler will do so. She brought him to your rooms early this morning, and she will collect him during the day while you attend the events." Her hand flicked toward me. "Please get out." She held up a long, thick white cloth. "We will dress, plus do your hair and make-up."

"Koko?"

"Will play with his littermates." She gave me a soft smile. "I promise he will be safe and happy."

Well, at least I didn't have to clean the litter box. I wasn't sure what I'd do with him when I left the fae kingdom, and I wasn't going to ask. I'd deal with it later.

"Quickly, now," she said. "It's time for you to attend breakfast, where you will interact with eligible bachelors."

Did I have to? I'd already met the bachelor I wanted.

Hold on. I sat up, not caring that I exposed my breasts—breasts that Elion had stroked last night.

I wasn't here to find a match. Getting back to my sister with lots of money was my goal. I needed to remember that.

With new resolve lighting a fire inside me, I let her help me dress in the pale-yellow gown that made me feel a bit like Belle in *Beauty and the Beast*.

"Sit," Maecia said, pointing to a chair parked in front of a mirror. She fluttered around me, not touching me but somehow arranging my hair in an elaborate up sweep that made me look like I had awesome cheekbones. She did the same thing with my face, flicking her fingers toward me as if bestowing fairy dust.

Elf dust, I supposed, since she was an elf.

"Done," she pronounced, standing back and looking me over with a critical eye. "Oh, earrings." A blink of her eyes, and a cluster of diamonds dangled from my ears. "Now, you are ready."

"We're just having breakfast, right? Why so fancy?" I asked, staring at my image in the mirror, bemused. I couldn't help wondering. What would Elion think of how I looked?

I growled, irritated at myself for caring what he thought. Yeah, he'd made me come. He had magical fingers. It meant nothing. I could keep my heart encased in steel.

"Each time you leave this room," Maecia said. "You are on display."

"I'm not a doll."

"No, you are not. You are a human woman who will soon make a fine fae match." She smiled benignly. "I am determined to do my part to see it done."

Don't try too hard. I bit back the words. My goal here was my secret. Revealing it could get me into trouble. When I initially agreed to take part in the drawing, I promised if I was chosen, I'd give this a fair chance.

Maecia clapped her hands, and her smile widened. "You look wonderful. We must hurry. You cannot be late."

I stopped at the bed to pat Koko, then followed Maecia.

She hustled me down the hall, my guard following. I'd climbed up the trellis the night before, skinning my right knee and nearly toppling backward while Elion fretted on the ground beneath me.

Frankly, I was worried I'd fall backward and crush him, but all was good. I'd reached the roof, and after a quick wave, slunk back inside my room with the guard completely unaware I'd left.

It was a good thing Maecia was with me now, or I'd

still be wandering around the castle at midnight, trying to find the breakfast room.

"Down here," she said, pointing to a long hall with many closed doors on each side. "And across this landing." She guided me down a flight of stairs and into yet another long hallway.

"How many rooms does the castle have?" I asked, amazed by the architecture, the paintings on the walls of mythical creatures, and the high gilded ceilings.

Maecia nodded to me but batted her eyelashes at the guard. "Four hundred and thirty-eight." Her fingers twitched at her sides, and the guard kept staring at Maecia's ass. I didn't blame him. She had a perfectly heart-shaped, cute ass.

"That's a lot of rooms," I said as Maecia took me down a long flight of stairs and onto what I believed was the first floor.

"It is indeed." She led me down another hall but paused outside an arched doorway at the end. Silverware clinked, and the low murmur of voices called out to me from inside.

Maecia bowed. "I will leave you now, but expect me in your rooms promptly at four to help you change for the evening."

I pinched my golden dress, pulling it away from my thigh. "What's wrong with this?"

"It will never do for dinner and dancing." With that, she turned and scurried away, sending flirtatious glances at the guard as she passed him.

While he stared after her, I entered the breakfast room.

They'd set a table for what looked like a hundred people, and three-quarters of the chairs were full, mostly with fae guys dressed in jackets in a variety of colors a-la Mr. Darcy.

Betts waved and pointed to the chair on her left. A fae dude sat on her right. His gaze lowered as if he was staring at her boobs.

I'd started across the room to join her when someone cleared their throat from the doorway.

"You will sit with me," he said in a low, husky voice.

I turned to find Elion watching me with a predatory gleam in his eyes.

Chapter 17
Elion

"Next time you come, it will be from my mouth," I said softly by Raven's ear. She'd come from my fingers last night, and I hadn't been able to think of anything else since.

Color rose into her face, and I took in how gorgeous she was dressed in fae finest. All the human women were beautiful in their own way, but Raven shone among them like the rarest of jewels.

I was falling for her, and I couldn't do a damn thing to keep it from happening. Would it be so bad to steal what I could for now, knowing my end was in sight?

One of her eyebrows lifted. "You assume I'll grant you a next time."

"There will be," I said with complete confidence. She had joined me outside last night. She'd followed me into the woods. Despite my assumption no one would ever look at me with favor, this female did.

It stunned me, and it was all I could do to maintain a controlled façade. I ached to take her from this place of dubious safety. Was there a place we could run to where no one would harm her?

My property, perhaps. I'd think about it.

Many of my former friends and current enemies watched us from their positions at the dining table. They knew I was not supposed to attend the events, that the humans had been forbidden to choose me.

For whatever reason, I suspected Raven was ignoring that rule.

None of the males rose to step between us, however. My face and body may be riddled with scars and my soul eternally cursed, but my formidable reputation remained undefeated.

I held out my arm. "If you are willing?" I made it a question and not the demand hovering on the tip of my tongue. Someone as independent as Raven would need to be coaxed. I'd made enough demands in the past I now regretted.

My ancestors would've said the hell with it and lulled her with magic, but I had my suspicions that was part of the reason I was cursed. I had not lulled another, but my now-dead father had done this often. And the fae woman he'd lulled before he was suddenly killed had—

"All right," Raven said, her face softening. She linked her hand through my arm, and I led her to two empty seats.

Unfortunately, Lady Axilya sat across from us. She

watched, her face unreadable, though I didn't need an expression to show me her thoughts. She'd speak with me later, and she'd remain polite in her demand that I stay away from Raven. As for her conversation with Raven, Axilya wouldn't make even the slightest effort to temper her words.

This, I would not allow, and my glare made it clear that if she came after Raven, she would find me standing in her path.

She huffed, showing my message had been received.

Once the king arrived, everyone ate, speaking of the upcoming events. A few whispered about the human who was found in the fountain last night, but we'd been told her death was an accident, and it was hard to maintain a thread of gossip from that.

I was not convinced, and the fact that the king had assigned guards to each woman showed he had his own suspicions about what happened.

The other males at the table outright stared at me, some shooting daggers with their eyes, others sneering. They didn't like that I usurped Raven's attention, and they'd complain to the king. What would my cousin say about that? He was one of the few who hadn't scorned me after I was cursed.

"You're not eating much," Raven said, nudging her chin toward my plate.

"I told you what I crave."

She laughed, low, deep, and a bit sultry. "You might want to eat from your plate, then. Just because you declared your intention, it doesn't mean I'm going to follow you back out into the garden."

She dared me, did she?

My cock twitched, and the feral part of me I kept bound stirred, suggesting I carry her from the room, find a secluded location, and show her how she made me come undone.

"We shall see," I bit out.

I picked at my food to justify my presence, but I heaved an internal sigh of relief when others started pushing their plates away, showing they were finished.

The king rose, smiling benignly. "I have matters to attend to this morning, but I look forward to attending the evening event." He dipped his head to each of the women, then left the room, his entourage hovering behind him. "Do enjoy yourselves today."

Lady Axilya stood, her gaze pointedly remaining off me. "Ladies."

She nodded to the five remaining humans. Fae women would not be invited to take part in any of the events, as the king would not wish to thrust competition into the mix.

"If you would follow me to the side foyer," Lady Axilya said. "I'd like to speak with each of you for a moment."

It was all she could do not to glare at Raven, whose conversation I'd usurped for the entire meal.

The men gathered to the side of the doorway, watching as the women left with Axilya.

Their hostility toward me was a toxic mist hanging in

the air. Ignoring them, I strode out into the hall, watching Raven walk away with the others.

The side foyer, then? What activity was on the agenda for this morning? I hadn't bothered to look but would obtain a schedule.

I'd gone from trying to avoid the events to a willing participant.

"You need to let this go," Nuvian said softly from beside me. I was so fixated on Raven that I hadn't heard him come near. He'd sat at the table beside one of the other humans, and while I'd felt his concerned gaze, I'd ignored his pointed stares.

"I cannot."

"You endanger her."

"Life in the fae kingdom endangers her more than me."

The women left the hall and proceeded toward the side foyer. Would they go outside or adjourn to one of the parlors after Axilya spoke with them?

Males who hoped to win them filed out of the room, each shooting sharp glares my way.

"You speak of what happened last night," Nuvian said.

"We know it was not an accident. Raven and I found her in the fountain. There were distinct marks on her neck that could not come from her fall."

"The king insists it was an accident." Warning rang out in his voice, but he wasn't threatening me, just giving me a warning. If I remained vocal, others would hear and speak up. Nuvian's loyalty remained with the king, as was right, but he would do all he could to keep me from getting into trouble.

"And I would never refute the king." I wouldn't let this go, however. I could remain quiet and still look into it.

"Do not distract me," Nuvian said, ignoring the males glaring at me as they left the dining room and headed toward the first event of the day. "Leave the castle. Go to your estate. Remain there until the women have all picked someone to marry. No, remain there until they are wedded, bedded, and expecting."

"I cannot," I said softly. I couldn't make myself look at my friend and advisor. "I've tried."

"You need to try harder. Being with her endangers her. You know this."

I pinched my eyes shut.

"Do not suck her into your curse."

"I have to believe it can be broken."

"I wish this for you as well." He leaned against the wall. "I understand why you pursue her, friend. She is lovely; unbelievably tempting."

A growl ripped through my chest.

Nuvian rolled his eyes. "Please. You know I will not pursue her."

"I don't want anyone to pursue her. I want . . ."

"What we all do. My heart longs to find my true mate, and I hope she is among the humans since I have not found her here in the kingdom."

"Raven is not my true mate." I snarled, but his words gave me pause. What if she *was* my true mate? That would explain why I couldn't stay away from her. She was all I'd thought of since I met her at the dining establishment where she worked.

"If she's not your true mate, why can't you let her go?" His perceptive gaze locked on mine.

"I don't know. I . . . I'm sorry. I know you mean well."

"I would die to protect you." He chuckled low, but the sound held no humor. "And I would die if the ending of my life would break your curse."

A chill passed through me. "Do not say that."

He pressed his fist against his chest. "I mean it. We've been friends since we were children."

My father had courted our friendship, bringing Nuvian into our home and training him to protect me as he grew older. This was a common thing among the fae aristocracy. Being raised closer than brothers ensured loyalty.

With gratitude pouring through my heart, I gripped his shoulders. "Thank you, but no one can break the curse but me."

I was even more grateful when he didn't shrug away from my touch like so many others. What had I done to deserve this friend? Not enough.

"Have you learned anything new about the curse?" he asked.

I turned and leaned against the wall beside him. "I found an ancient scroll in the castle library."

His lips twisted. "An ancient scroll speaking of your curse happened to be lying about in the library?"

"It wasn't lying about. I . . . I found a hidden bookcase

behind a wall. Most of the scrolls inside told me nothing, but one suggested—"

"What?"

"That if a cursed fae could find love everlasting, and such a person was willing to sacrifice, a spell like mine can be broken."

Chapter 18
Raven

My spine tingled, telling me Elion was staring at me.

He and Nuvian strode across the back deck of the castle and took the broad, sweeping staircase to the path leading across the lawn. They joined the large cluster of lords staring at me and my friends along the side of the game field, though Elion hung back while Nuvian greeted the others.

I'd be clueless not to notice that many scorned him. Did he have any friends here other than Nuvian? It didn't appear so. I felt bad, but even more, I felt furious. It wasn't my job to protect him, but I found myself aching to do so.

"Gather near, ladies," Axilya said, shooting me a look of warning. She'd pinned me in the foyer and told me to beware. That was it, just "beware". I believe the only reason she hadn't ripped me a new one was because I'd also caught the glare of warning Elion sent her at the breakfast table. "I need to explain the rules of this game."

"It looks vaguely like croquet to me," Betts whispered as we joined the other women standing with Lady Axilya. Her long blue skirt swished around her ankles, and her hair was secured tight against the back of her head, making her eyes look permanently widened.

I'd chuckle if I wasn't worried that I looked the same.

I took in the hoops magically suspended above the ground and the roundish creatures clustered together near golden mallets hovering mid-air.

"Each of you will collect a living ball and golden mallet," Axilya said.

"I'm not hitting a *living* ball with any mallet, golden or otherwise," Rhaelyn said, shifting her hips to the side and propping her fist on one hip. She wore a formal gown like me, and the rich green color made her gorgeous brown skin pop.

"The wooferines have been contracted for the event," Axilya said, a bit shrilly. "And you *will* hit them. That is the point of the game. You must move your wooferine through the rings and around the course with as few hits as possible and before the butterflies stop you."

"Why would butterflies want to stop us?" I asked, cringing like Rhaelyn at the thought of hitting a living being through a ring. I didn't care if they were contracted to do this. The mallets looked hard enough to leave bruises.

"Because they are also under contract," Lady Axilya said. "Without conflict, there is no game. All of you will pick a partner—from the fae lords waiting along the sidelines, please—and compete. Whoever wins the event will be awarded a small estate in the mountains of Vustine, one of the loveliest parts of the kingdom."

"A freakin' estate?" Betts blurted out. "Just for winning a game?"

"Language, my dear," Axilya scolded. "We do not use profanity, especially when we hope to impress."

"That's not what I'm seeing," Betts whispered, leaning close to me. "Aillun had no problem telling me he'd be eager to fuck me during a dance last night. Creep."

Aillun might be heir to the throne, but he sure didn't act princely. Although, many of the royalty through the human ages hadn't acted any better than him.

I wasn't the only one who cringed when they felt the weight of his hawklike stare. I'd quickly realized he was the one sitting sneering on the balcony when we arrived. He might act like he was willing to marry one of us, but I got the feeling his polite façade would disappear the moment the ring was on our finger.

Lady Axilya clapped her hands. "Quickly now. Choose your partner and select a mallet and wooferine. It's time for the game to get started."

"I don't care if they give me a castle," Rhaelyn said. "I'm not hitting one of those furry brown things with a mallet."

I contemplated joining Rhaelyn's burgeoning coup, but Axilya's glare made me reconsider. I was on thin ice with her already.

Rhaelyn sighed and walked over to pick a fae guy to compete with us. I followed. Maybe one of them could suggest a way to play the game without smacking a fluffy wooferine. As for the butterflies, they'd yet to make an appearance, but I had my doubts a small insect could make a difference.

I studied the guys as I strolled toward them. Betts quickly chose Nuvian, a surprise, as I didn't think she'd noticed him. The other women also paired up, leaving only me to decide. The thirty or so fae lords stood, a few scowling, the rest bowing and smiling.

There wasn't anyone other than Elion I wanted to choose, and from the sharp looks one or two of the fae men sent him, they knew.

Hard to be second best, guys.

Elion brooded; his muscular arms linked across his chest. He remained back, away from the others.

"Hurry," Axilya cried. "The butterflies will arrive soon, and they'll be hungry."

Hungry? I gulped, peering toward the sky, but seeing nothing.

I couldn't pick anyone but Elion. To put off being forced to do so, I deviated my path and strode over to collect a mallet. When I touched one of them, magically dangling in the air, it snarled.

Shit, the mallet was alive too.

"Be that way," I said, clutching my fingers to my throat.

"Only one is meant for you," Elion said from behind me.

As I turned, my heel caught on something, and I stumbled.

He reached out and tugged me close, keeping me from falling and reminding me of what happened last night. My skin still quivered from the power of that orgasm. It wasn't fair that a guy could make my body respond like that.

Make? I'd been willing. No, I'd practically thrown myself at him, and given another chance, I'd do it again. I'd not only climb his luscious body, but I'd also let him do whatever he pleased with mine.

So much for my determination to avoid him.

He eased me away from his body. "Pick a different mallet. You'll know it is meant for you when it warms."

I was warming up already, something that happened whenever Elion came near. I walked from one mallet to the next, Elion following.

"Won't you get in trouble for hanging out with me?" I asked.

"I do as I please."

Must be nice. "I've been warned."

He shot a glare Axilya's way. "You may also do as you please."

I huffed, but I didn't say anything more about that. The rules might not apply to *Lord* Elion, but they sure as hell did to me.

One of the mallets hummed when I came near. I didn't hear it; I more sensed the vibration in my bones. When I wrapped my fingers around it, it heated.

"See?" Elion whispered by my ear. "This is yours."

My smut brain heard, *I am yours,* but there was nothing real about that. He didn't want more than some fun, and I was leaving the kingdom as soon as I reasonably could.

"Great. Now all I need to do is pick my partner."

Numerous fae men crowded closer, like this was the supermarket's deli, and they'd all had the tag with the next number.

"Haven't you already chosen?" A world of meanings came through in Elion's voice. While he smiled with confidence, his hands twitched. Did he expect me to reject him in front of his peers?

I shouldn't do this. I *really* shouldn't do this. But I couldn't seem to help myself.

"Lord Elion? Would you like to help me win this game?"

He flashed me a bone-melting grin. "I'd be delighted."

The fae guys coming near grumbled and groaned and returned to take seats along the side of the course.

Elion and I joined the others waiting for the event to start.

"What do we do?" I asked.

"We hit the wooferines, aiming to get through the course as quickly as possible." He held out his hand for the mallet. "Would you like me to go first?"

"You said the mallet was only meant for me."

"We are paired for the game. That means it will permit me *anything*."

Damn, he could make a woman swoon with just a

few words. I knew very well what he suggested—that *I'd* also permit him anything.

He was probably right. Despite my determination to hold myself back, I was falling under his spell.

"Are you using magic on me?" I asked, as I gave him the mallet.

"I am not." He could be lying, but I sensed the sincerity in his words.

In many ways, this would be easier for me if he was. Then I could find a way to break his spell and avoid him after that.

Instead, I was trapped with no way out. My heart had thrown itself into this game between us, and it was anyone's guess who'd win.

He surveyed the course and smacked the wooferine with the mallet. It soared forward, and the ball actually giggled. My tension eased. The wooferines truly didn't mind playing this game.

Others took their turns, and I began to believe the threats of killer butterflies were only something to make us try harder.

Until something soared over my head from behind and snatched Betts's wooferine out of the air. I gaped as a butterfly the size of a large dog flapped its bright pink wings. It flew toward the forest with the wooferine in its clutches.

Betts crumpled, though Nuvian caught and steadied her. "My wooferine," she wailed. "That damn butterfly stole it."

"Will the butterfly eat the wooferine?" I asked, cringing.

"No, it will release it," Elion said. He handed me the mallet. "We must hurry, though. More will be here soon and our wooferine and the prize are in danger."

My good mood popped. "You're only doing this to win a prize?"

He leaned in close. "Oh, no, little human. I've already chosen my prize, and it's you."

Chapter 19
Raven

After we finished the game—and Rhaelyn won—Axilya shepherded us to the castle. Lord Elion followed, but Nuvian grabbed his arm, holding him back. They spoke in hushed, though heated tones, as I stepped inside the building.

"We will have a light repast," Axilya said, her voice echoing in the large, ornate entryway. "And then we will begin the next event." She clapped her hands. "Follow me!"

"I can't help noticing that you and Lord Elion are becoming a thing," Betts said. When the door opened and a group of fae men stepped inside, she glanced toward them. I didn't need to look. I sensed his presence coming closer. "You need to be careful. He's forbidden."

"Why?" I asked. "I mean, Camile warned me away, Axilya, too, but no one seems to want to give me the fine details as to why he's strictly forbidden. He's a lord; he should be equally up for grabs."

"Is that what you want, to grab him?"

My lips thinned. "You know what I mean."

"I do, but you need to be careful. I've . . . heard things."

How could she hear anything I wasn't privy to? "Like what."

"He's cursed."

"Camile told me that the day we arrived," I said.

"And you didn't listen to her warning?" She shivered, her arms snaking around her waist. "This isn't *Beauty and the Beast*. We're not in a haunted castle with a bunch of pots and pans, determined to break the curse." She shook her head. "Although, you're cute. Him, not so much, but I can see how his rough edges might hold appeal."

"I'm well aware this isn't a fairytale."

Betts chuckled until she noted I was serious. "The thing is, I've heard he'll die within a year."

"All the more reason to make each second matter."

"Oh, you've got it bad."

I wanted to protest that, of course, I didn't have it bad, but she was right. While I was still very much determined to leave here within three months, I wasn't so determined to leave Elion. "I barely know him."

"Sometimes, you don't need to know someone long to know they're the one." She said it sadly, and I wondered if she spoke from personal experience.

"Ladies," Axilya called out before I could say anything more. She tipped her head, sending daggers our way with her sharp gaze. "Come along, please."

We hurried across the foyer and followed the other

women down a hall, entering another parlor, this one decorated in silver from the tassels on the sofa cushions to the gilding on the walls. Even the linens draped on the "repast" buffet table gleamed like polished steel.

"I'm sorry if you've been hurt," I said softly as we milled behind the other women lining up for the buffet line.

"Life sucks, but you can either wallow in it or shrug it off. I chose the latter." She peered over her shoulder. "He's following you, you know."

I knew the second he entered the room; I could feel his heavy gaze on my spine.

"I can tell him to take off if he's pestering you," she added as we took tiny plates and started loading them with food.

"He's not and don't."

"Okay. I warned you. Whatever you do now is on you."

It had always been on me.

I lowered my plate on the table and sat, noting Elion speaking with Nuvian on the other side of the room.

Betts dropped into the seat beside me. "I mean, I understand. A cursed, tragic hero. Magic swirling in the air. We're in the fae kingdom. If someone hideous like him looked at me like he does you, I have to admit I'd be more than tempted."

"He's not hideous," I said, affronted.

Her eyebrows shot up. "You've got it bad."

"I don't." I shoved a pale green, intricately decorated thing I assumed was a pastry into my mouth and gagged.

How could something that tasted like vomit be so pretty? I coughed and delicately spit it out into my napkin.

Axilya frowned at me from the end of the long table, but she thankfully said nothing.

"If you don't have it bad, you won't have a problem staying away from him, then," Betts said.

I pushed away my plate, not daring to try anything else. "Why do you care?"

Her face fell. "I'm just being friendly. After what happened to Crystal, the rest of us need to watch out for each other. I don't want to see you hurt."

I shuddered at the memory of Crystal lying in the water. "I'm sorry I snapped."

"It's okay," she said. "Just . . . be careful, okay? There's one more thing I heard about him."

"What's that?" I washed down the bitter taste of the green thing with the beverage one of the elf staffers had poured for me.

"I heard something horrible could happen to anyone who gets close to him. There's a witch involved, I think." She grunted. "And I can't believe I just made that statement. A year ago, the only witches I ran into were those in costumes on Halloween."

"I'm not worried about anything like that."

Feeling the weight of someone's gaze, I studied those in the room.

Elion still spoke with Nuvian and wasn't looking my way. Everyone else was eating and talking.

Only the portrait of a stern-appearing woman hanging on the wall across from me seemed to peer in this direction, but eyes in paintings always seemed to follow you.

"I'll be careful, thanks," I said, staring at the woman's eyes. Her rich brown hair hung past her shoulders, and she wore a bright red gown that revealed the tops of her boobs. An ice-encrusted castle had been painted behind her, looming on a cliff with a stormy sea beyond.

Betts nodded pertly and continued eating.

I couldn't stop thinking about her words. Could curses be real? Although, we were talking about the fae kingdom. I'd already seen magic.

"Why do you think he's cursed?" I asked Betts.

"No idea. I could ask Nuvian for more deets if you want."

That felt intrusive. "It's okay. It doesn't matter."

Her laugh snorted out. "Sure."

I laughed because she was right. Giving into my humor made the heavy feeling in the air disappear.

We finished, and Axilya took us through more castle halls than I could keep track of.

"For our next event," she said, opening a door and stepping out onto a stone deck with a broad lawn beyond. "We will ride glisteers. Come now, the herd is waiting."

Betts joined me on the deck, and we gaped at the creatures waiting to give us a ride.

The size of elephants, their teal blue leathery skin almost gleamed in the sunlight. They shifted their hooves and nudged each other with huge horns jutting up off their heads. Their horns curled around and around, the ends pointing forward in vicious appearing spikes. Their lighter blue manes and tails rippled in the breeze, and one creature stretched out its long trunk toward Betts.

She gulped and stepped back until she ran into the outer wall of the castle. "I don't ride."

"We *all* ride," Axilya said sternly. "Come along. Choose a partner from among the lords, and he will select your mount. No worries. You'll ride as a pair, and these creatures are very tame."

"Yeah, sure," Betts said.

"Quickly, now," Axilya said. "We will ride sedately along the trails and gather together after a lovely ride for a small party deep within the forest. There will be dancing." She clapped her hands again, something I was heartily sick of already. "Hurry!"

Betts approached Nuvian, who shook his head and remained beside Elion. Elion watched the beasts, not watching me. Her lips souring, Betts strode up to another fae lord, who bowed and took her hand. They left the deck and crossed the lawn toward the glisteers.

Soon, all the women had chosen a riding partner. The rest of the lords stared at me.

I should pick one of them, flirt, and then cut away from him before the dancing. But fuck it. Betts was right; I couldn't seem to resist Elion.

I strode over to him and held out my hand. "Would you like to ride a glisteer with me?"

Chapter 20
Elion

"Don't do it," Nuvian hissed, keeping his voice low. Raven heard him, and her face reddened. Her shoulders began to curl forward, and despite his warning and everything inside me telling me it would be wrong to give into my desire, I took her hand.

Nuvian's glare rode my spine as Raven and I left the deck and approached the saddled glisteers. The one I selected shifted its hooves and blew softly.

"Allow me to help you mount," I said.

"Sure." Raven gaped at the creature. "Do they bite?"

"No, but they have been known to stab those who irritate them with their horns."

She backed away from the head of the beast. "Then let's not irritate them."

"They are sedate creatures most of the time. The odds of that happening are slim."

"If you say so."

I spanned her waist with my hands.

"You can't—" Her words dissolved into a yelp as I lifted her easily up onto the beast, seating her in the front of the double saddle. "Well, okay." Her hands flailed a bit before she grabbed a clump of the beast's mane.

I leaped up behind her, settling close to her delectable ass, and pried her fingers from the mane. "This irritates them."

She flung her hands up in horror. "Fuck."

My laugh snorted out. "So soon, little human?" I took her hands and lowered them to the grip on the front of the saddle.

"Ha, ha."

It would be so easy to lure her, to whisper words in her ear that would enthrall her forever. Lords used to do this with humans in the past. They'd call them to the woods and seduce them, then leave them to wander home on their own.

No matter how much I craved Raven, I could never do this to her. If she came to me, it would be with free will.

The other glisteers meandered toward the trail, their riders swaying in the saddles. My gaze met Nuvian's. He stood on the deck, gripping the rail hard enough to crush it.

I tapped a finger to my forehead. I'd be fine without his protection for a short while. This was a large group. While the glisteers may be docile with us, they were ferocious if threatened. Nothing would come near us.

"You're sure this beast won't buck us off?" Raven asked, her voice tight.

"It will not."

"Okay, good." She settled back against me, and my body responded like dry tinder with a spark. "You're um . . . Yeah." Her ass wiggled.

"If you keep that up, you will drive me out of my mind."

She shot me a heavy glance over her shoulder, but at least she stopped shifting against my cock. "How do you behave when you're out of your mind?"

"You do not wish to know."

"Perhaps I do. Some women enjoy being wild and feral."

We played a dangerous game. Was she aware of the consequences? Hell, was I?

"What about you?" I asked.

Her voice dropped to almost nothing. "Oh, yes, I do enjoy being feral."

My cock was on fire. She couldn't miss it pressing against her spine. But the others rode with us, and the last thing I needed to do was let on how much this woman was coming to mean to me.

"Behave," I said.

She just chuckled.

"We're eating dust," she finally said, waving to the dust clouding the air. "I guess there's nothing we can do about it, though."

There was. Did I dare take this risk? In my heart, I was all in. There was no stopping the feral part of me from rushing forward and plunging off the cliff. Did I dare risk taking her with me?

I had to trust the curse could be broken, and that Raven was the one who could do it.

That thought convinced me to let the fates guide me.

When we reached a fork in the path, the rest of the group went right. I directed our glisteer to the left. With the sun shining, and mounted on a glisteer, I wasn't worried about flazires. *She* wouldn't dare send her demons when someone else might witness. No, she was a coward at heart. She'd only attack when I was alone.

I didn't know why she pursued me so relentlessly. Wasn't her curse enough?

"We need to stay with the others, don't we?" Raven asked, her fingers tightening on the saddle horn.

"We can join up with them later. Are you afraid of being alone with me, little human?"

She stilled before she relaxed back against me. "Why should I be?"

"Because you're alone with the true beast of the castle."

Leaning forward, she patted the glisteer's neck. "Don't talk like that about someone so cute."

"I meant me," I growled near her ear.

"So did I."

That made me pause. "I am not cute," I scoffed.

"You're right," she sighed. "You're not traditionally cute."

I shouldn't feel upset by that statement. She didn't say anything others hadn't repeated ad nauseam until their scorn had embedded itself in my skin.

"You're gorgeous, actually," she said softly.

"You don't need to . . . kiss up. That's the human term for what you said, correct?"

When she peered back at me, I was struck by the honesty shining in her eyes. I couldn't look away. "Why do you think I'm lying?"

Unwilling to let her read my expression, I turned my head to peer into the woods along the trail. "You are no different from all the others." I said this, but in my heart, I knew it was untrue. She *was* different. Perfect. Unobtainable. Yet I couldn't stop from craving her company.

"Now you're the one lying." She laid her hand on my arm that encircled her waist. When had I placed it there?

"I speak the truth."

"And so do I." With a huff, she settled against me again. Her fingers teased across my arm, and I did nothing to stop it. "You live in the castle?"

Perhaps we needed to change the conversation. Frustration built inside me, and if it continued, I'd explode. I wasn't irritated with Raven. No, the witch was the reason I wasn't standing among the fawning lords, hoping for a touch of Raven's hand. Her curse excluded me from everything. I only half lived, and I'd never be whole.

"I have rooms in the castle," I said. "But I also have estates in the mountains." Ice covered since the curse, but I'd learned to accept that.

"What's it like in the mountains?" The eagerness shining in her voice told me she didn't ask just to make conversation. She truly wanted to know.

"Cold. Harsh. Forbidding. Beautiful."

"You like it there."

"How did you know?"

"I can hear it in your voice."

"I don't go there often." Not since the curse was laid upon me. Everyone fled after it happened, and walking the dark halls alone only made me sadder. I'd lost something that could never be replaced, and per the curse, I'd never find it.

Except . . . Could I do so with Raven?

"Why stay in the castle if you love it so much?"

"It calls to me, but I need others around me." They kept me from sinking into despair.

"I guess I understand that."

We rode longer, taking the trail deeper into the woods. Our conversation varied from our favorite foods to which season we loved above all others. She spoke of her mother's death, and the gut-wrenching pain in her voice made me hold her tighter. If I could, I'd protect her from everything.

But I couldn't even protect her from me.

"Now it is only you and your sister," I said.

"Yes, that's why I have to . . ."

I could guess what she didn't say. Before she came here, she'd made up her mind. She wouldn't match with anyone. She'd return as soon as the king allowed.

Could I bear to watch her go? If I was a decent person, I wouldn't keep pursuing her.

Was it so bad to try to steal a bit of her wonder for myself?

The forest brightened, and the glisteer strode out into a meadow overrun with wistella flowers.

Raven's breath caught. "It's so pretty."

"They're weeds."

"Even weeds serve a purpose. Can we get down?"

The slant of the sun told me we had hours left before we must return to the castle. "Of course."

I dismounted, then lifted her off, lowering her carefully to her feet.

She wandered around the meadow, stopping to pick flowers. She sat in the deep grass, kicked off her heels to expose her toes, and tugged her skirts up above her knees. She had lovely legs. I wanted to touch them. Lick them.

Completely unaware of the lust consuming me, she laid the flowers in her lap and proceeded to coil them into a wreath.

I watched her until she patted the ground at her side. "You're looming."

"I apologize." I joined her, trying desperately not to notice how beautiful she was with the sun lighting up her hair and kissing her freckled cheeks. Others might note her too-slender nose or the pert point to her chin. One tooth in the front that was slightly crooked. Her lush shape and her often stiff shoulders. The intelligence gleaming in her eyes.

She was the loveliest being I'd ever seen, and I'd be a fool not to claim her.

Did I dare?

I'd begun to believe it was too late. She'd thawed the ice lord, and as long as I remained near her, I might never harden again.

She rose to her knees and laid the crown on the top of my head. "There. I crown you king."

"Ice king?"

"You're not cold, Elion." She tightly gripped my shoulders. "Maybe with others, but not with me."

I wasn't surprised she'd seen past my wall. Some believed when the fae met their true mates, they couldn't hide anything from the one they'd adore.

I no longer wished to hide from Raven.

With a groan, I tugged her close. I watched her face, but I'd yet to find rejection. When her lips parted, I devoured them, gliding my tongue across hers while she moaned and clung.

Soon, she lay on the ground with me over her.

When I lifted my head, she stared at me with languid wonder. I couldn't resist this little human, and I would no longer try.

Watching her face, I slowly bunched up her skirt, sliding it along her thighs.

I waited for her to tell me no.

All she did was glide her tongue across her lips

And part her thighs.

Chapter 21
Raven

Was I crazy to give into this moment? With heat searing through my veins, this felt inevitable. Destined. Right.

I couldn't hold myself back.

I didn't know where this was going, and there was no way to tell how this might affect me leaving the fae kingdom, but I couldn't deny my needs.

I couldn't deny *him*.

His fingers trailed up my inner thigh in a tickling heat. My bones sighed, and I relaxed my legs further.

With my skirts fluffed around my waist, I relaxed on the grass. A light breeze tickled my exposed skin.

Elion eased my panties down and moved in close. While his breath teased my exposed flesh, he ran his thumb down my crease. It glided because I was wet for him already.

His groan slipped out, turning into a growl. He shouldered his way between my legs and laid his mouth on my clit.

Flames shot through me as he sucked it into his mouth and nibbled on it with his teeth.

I was a writhing mess already, and he'd barely touched me.

He slid a finger inside me and pumped it while I panted and fisted the grass, ripping some of it up. While he added another finger and moved faster, his tongue coiled around my clit. My cry of pleasure echoed in the small meadow.

His low chuckle vibrated through my pelvic bones, and he licked and sucked harder. While his fingers fucked me, his tongue drove me closer to the edge.

My orgasm hit me, unexpected and oh so fulfilling. I rocked against his fingers that moved faster, pushing me to explode once more.

I collapsed in the grass, a limp wreck, and he rose above me. He stared down at me, his eyes dark with pure satisfaction. Lying beside me, he held me, stroking my shoulders and teasing his fingers where my flesh was exposed above the bodice of my dress.

My breathing slowed, and my mind kicked in, asking me what had just happened. I shoved the thought aside and decided to live for this moment. Questions about what this meant—if anything—could come later when I was alone in my room.

I may have dozed. It was hard to say. I woke suddenly to the cry of a bird in the distance.

"We have to go," he said.

"Truly? I'm not sure I want to." I marveled at how husky my voice sounded. We were so close to being lovers I could taste it, and I still wanted more.

His laugh rang out, relaxed and filled with the unfettered joy I hadn't heard from him yet. I liked that I could give him this, that he could find happiness in something so simple. "I'd love to lie here for days, but Nuvian will send guards if I don't return soon. Your friends will worry."

Reality stepped back into this magical moment, but it wasn't unexpected. I didn't know where whatever was developing between us would go next, and I wasn't going to ask. I'd take it as it came and savor each moment.

Elion was helping ease my underwear back up my legs when the cry of the bird I heard earlier echoed in the meadow. His fingers stilled, and he shot a worried look toward the trees.

A pale purple bird, like the one I'd seen when I first arrived, perched on one of the upper branches. When it saw us looking, it shrieked and dove toward the meadow.

Elion hissed and jerked to his feet, pulling me up. He nudged me behind him.

The bird landed on the grass and changed . . .

An elderly woman with long gray hair, wearing a deep purple cloak that brushed across her bare feet, leaned on a knobby cane, glaring at us.

I held onto Elion's waist and leaned around to watch her as she shambled closer.

The glisteer stomped its hooves and bellowed, a terror-filled sound that ground through my bones.

"This is forbidden," the woman shrieked, lumbering toward us using the support of her twisted branch cane.

"True love never is," Elion said softly. "Don't you see? You can't stop us."

"Oh no?" she cackled, the sound raising my hackles. "Watch me."

As her hand swirled and dingy yellow mist drifted from her fingers, he urged me over to the glisteer. Its wide, feral gaze and switching tail told me it was ready to bolt. It would leave without us.

I didn't know what Elion meant when he said true love except in a part deep of my heart that fluttered at his words. We barely knew each other, yet . . .

He was so easy to love.

"And her," the woman cried, flicking more murky yellow mist our way. Was it magic? If so, I had a feeling it would burn us. "Her past is catching up to her. If she's not careful, *she'll* have to pay the price."

The price of what? This must be the witch who'd cursed him, and now she threatened me.

I swallowed, but the lump of dread in my throat wouldn't go down.

Elion tossed me onto the glisteer and swung up behind me, his arm going around my waist to keep me safe. The beast whirled and raced from the meadow, hitting the trail at a run. Branches smacked my face as if the witch beat me for daring to reach for something that could never be mine.

Behind us, the witch cackled again. A movement overhead drew my eye. Beyond the upper branches swaying like a storm churned through the forest, I spied her flying in her bird form.

I didn't believe in magic, huh? It looked like magic had called my bluff.

"That's her, isn't it?" I asked.

"Who?"

"Don't play me. The witch who cursed you."

He didn't answer for so long, I didn't think he would. "What do you know about my curse?"

"Not enough. You need to tell me."

"I . . . Later."

It wasn't enough, but now wasn't the time to talk. My heart thudded like a fleeing herd of horses galloped through my chest, and my skin crawled with fear.

Thunder boomed overhead, followed by lightning and pouring rain. We were soaked through in seconds.

Elion leaned over me, sheltering me with his body. His arms remained around me, keeping me from falling as the glisteer galloped through the forest.

A bone-chilling shriek was followed by others, then multiple thuds racing up behind us.

Elion swore and urged the glisteer to run faster. Its sides heaved and lather dripped from its mouth.

Just when I thought whatever chased us would leap on us and drag us from our mount, the glisteer burst from the forest and raced across the lawn. It joined the others milling about without riders.

As fast as the storm started, it dissipated, clouds fleeing across the sky to reveal the late-day sunlight. The ground behind us steamed. Beneath our feet, it was as dry as a dead monk's bones.

The rest of our party had already returned. If Axilya discovered I'd left the pack, I would be in deep trouble, but even that thought didn't chill me.

I was worried about what the witch would do to Elion next.

Before the glisteer came to a full stop, Elion slid off its back, taking me to the ground with him. He swept me up and bolted for the castle, not stopping until he'd slammed the door behind us.

We stood in the foyer, dripping.

"You need to change. I'll get you to your rooms," he said, his voice deadened. I had a feeling if I pressed him for answers, he'd fully withdraw.

Our precious moment in the meadow was lost, stomped beneath the feet of a witch. I wanted to rage and try to retake what I'd lost, but I was scared.

What had she meant about my past catching up and me having to pay the price?

Nuvian stepped from the hall and into the foyer, a scowl embedded in his face. He said nothing, though he didn't have to. His scorn whipped me like the branches had as our glisteer raced through the forest.

Without a word, he opened a door on our right that led to a back stairwell. When he started climbing, we followed.

I wanted to question Elion about everything, but I refused to speak in front of Nuvian.

We reached my floor and Nuvian led us to my rooms.

"When can we talk?" I whispered to Elion.

Nuvian shot a growl over his shoulder. "There will be no talking. He needs to leave."

"I decide that." Elion snapped. "You overstep."

Pausing for a few seconds, Nuvian eventually jerked his head forward in an angry bow.

"I can spare a few minutes," Elion said in an even tone as he opened my door and led me inside. He shut the panel in Nuvian's face.

I moved forward, putting space between us. To demand answers, I couldn't be near him. Otherwise, I'd be tempted to drag him to my bed even with Nuvian stomping back and forth in the hall outside.

Something caught my attention by one of my windows, and I stepped in that direction, frowning. A large lump lay on the floor. The sun finally parted the last bit of clouds and light shot in through my window, outlining the lump.

My guttural cry rang out.

Madison Jacobson, the woman with the crisp British accent and blonde pageboy haircut, lay on my floor, unmoving. The deep slice across her throat and blood pooling around her told me she was killed only a short time ago.

After the witch flew above us in the forest?

My hands clutched to my mouth, I spun to face Elion, finding him staring at the wall above my bed.

You're Next was scrawled in red—Madison's blood?

As I gaped, it disappeared, melting into the surface.

Chapter 22
Elion

Raven cried out. Her hands bunched the fabric of her skirt as her wild gaze met mine. "They . . . Someone killed her. Just like Crystal, which was not a fuckin' accident, someone killed Madison and now they're going to kill me!"

I would not allow that to happen.

Nuvian burst into the room. He skidded to a stop when he saw Madison's body.

"Get out of here," he bellowed, grabbing my arm. "Both of you. Go to . . . Fuck, I don't know. Elion. Take her to your rooms. Lock the door, bespell it, and don't leave there until I come for you." He strode closer to Madison, though I noted he took care not to step in the blood. His arms lifted to chest height, and a pale blue mist drifted off his hands, landing on her still body.

We stood, gaping.

"Go," Nuvian yelled again. "I need to take care of this before . . ."

It was too late. How was he going to hide this from the king? Assuming that was his goal here.

I took Raven's hand and tugged her away from the gruesome scene. Two of the humans had been murdered.

And Raven had been marked next.

When we entered the hall, we ran into guards running down the corridor, followed by two of the other women who must've heard Raven's and Nuvian's raised voices.

One woman hurried over to Raven and put her arm around her shoulder. "Where were you? When we got back, you weren't with us." Her attention fell on me, and her brows narrowed.

She knew very well where we were. Off by ourselves. Together.

"We got lost," Raven said. Her gaze met mine, seeking confirmation.

"Yes, our glisteer bolted. We only now returned."

"You're okay?" the other woman asked, still frowning at me.

"I'm not," Raven said. Her hand lifted, pointing to her room, and her body trembled. "Madison's . . ." Turning into my chest, she clung to my shirt, quivering. She was going into shock, and I needed to get her somewhere safe.

Where was safe, though? Not in the hall. Not in my rooms. There was no safe place within the castle or in the woods beyond.

"What's up with Madison?" the other woman asked. Before I could tell her to wait, she rushed through the doorway. She came to a shuddering stop and reeled backward, flailing as she sped from the room. "Oh my God, she's dead." Her hands clawed at her throat. "She's dead!"

"Koko," Raven cried. She broke free of my embrace and ran into the room. "Koko. Koko!"

I raced after her, finding her frozen, staring at Madison. Nuvian had magicked away all the blood and the slice in the woman's neck.

It didn't surprise me that he'd done this. He always looked after King Khaidill's best interest, and a murdered woman—two, in fact—would destroy our fragile truce with the humans.

Madison lay on the floor, her hands clasped on her chest. A bruise had formed on her right temple, and if I knew our healers, they'd soon declare she'd fallen, hit her head on the windowsill, and died from the blow. A head injury. Another accident.

Only we three and the king would be aware she was murdered.

"Your resha kit is not here," Nuvian said, all pleasant-like. He strolled over to join us and shepherded us from the room, shutting the door. "I imagine the sweet kit is with a handler."

"That's right. Maecia told me someone would care for him while I was busy." Raven swallowed hard, her eyes darting to her door. She lowered her voice. "What did you do?"

"Nothing," Nuvian said, brushing past us. He met the king striding down the hall.

The remaining human women clustered together, their attention flicking from us to Raven's door.

"I want more guards," I told one of the elves standing nearby. "Post them outside my rooms and on the grounds beneath."

"Of course, sir," the elf guard said. He dipped forward before hurrying down the hall. The new detail would be posted before we reached my rooms.

"What do you think happened?" Raven's friend asked, twisting Raven's arm.

"She's dead," she whispered, looking at me. She wet her lips with her tongue. "I don't know what happened."

That much was true. She must sense Nuvian wanted to hide the truth, but it was stupid to bother now. Word would spread. Two women dying suddenly and of natural causes? Few would believe it.

And the killer would soon strike again.

The king strode up to the door and cracked it open, slipping inside without exposing the body. His son, Aillun, followed, his mouth a grim slash on his face.

As Aillun was shutting the door, his gaze flicked from mine to Raven. In his dark gaze, I swore I read satisfaction.

Chapter 23
Raven

When the king emerged from my room, he strode past us, his son at his side. "Follow."

Nuvian joined us, shutting the door.

We'd started after the king when Rhaelyn cried out behind us. "I want to go home. I'm bailing on this piece of shit deal."

I held tight to Elion's hand, worried someone would wrench me from his grasp.

"I don't want to stay either," Nashio said. "Get me out of this hellhole."

"Only Betts left." I pushed out a sigh. "And me." And I had no idea what I wanted to do. I should leave, right? Someone had marked me for death and let's face it, as a magic-less person, there wasn't anything I could do to stop them.

My knees shook, and I kept swallowing back bile. All I could see was Madison lying on the floor with her throat cut. The blood . . .

Elion studied my face, but I didn't dare ask him what he hoped to see.

If all the other women left, how could I stay here alone? To think I'd been eager to leave before I even got here. Now leaving felt like I would rip away one of my limbs.

Love shouldn't slam into a person like this.

The king turned. His growl ripped through the room, and his glare took in the gaping audience of guards, staff, and the women. "I would like to speak with all of you in the green library." He pivoted and strode down the hall with his son and his full detail of guards hurrying behind him.

We crowded inside the big room aptly named the green library since plants had taken over most of the open spaces, and long rows of books covered two walls.

The king sat in an oversized wooden chair with spikes jutting up from the back. It was mounted in front of a huge desk and on a gilded platform.

Elion guided me farther into the room and urged me to sit on a green floral sofa.

Rhaelyn and Nashio leaned against the wall inside the entrance, and Betts followed Nuvian over to join me and Elion, though he gave her a pointed look and took a chair. She stared at him long enough that it made me uncomfortable before sitting on a matching sofa that also faced the king's desk.

"What is this nonsense about leaving?" He may project calm, but his icy stare shouted out his fury. He leaned back in the chair and clasped his hands on his chest.

Aillun took a position behind him with the ever-alert guards lining the back and side walls.

"Women are dying," Rhaelyn growled.

Nashio nodded and eased closer to Rhaelyn.

"Two accidents," King Khaidill said. "Two tragedies that must not compromise the treaty."

"This is about more than the treaty," Rhaelyn said.

"I, too, am horrified that they've died. Here. In the castle!"

"What happens if another one of us dies by . . . accident?" she asked. "Will you then agree something terrifying is happening here and let us go home?"

"They were accidents."

She huffed. "Show me the coroner's report."

"Our healers are more than able to determine the cause of death," he said. "We speak of magic."

"And that's the problem. What magical things are happening when you're not watching?" she said.

His fingers twitched. "You agreed to remain here for three months. You've only been here a few days."

"That was before someone died!"

Aillun stepped forward, his gaze pinning Rhaelyn in place. "Enough. No one speaks in such a manner to the king. You are here by his grace alone."

Not Aillun's, who'd made it clear he wasn't happy we were here. Although, as Betts pointed out, he'd be happy to fuck us.

"I'm sorry." Rhaelyn's lips thinned. "I don't mean to shout. I'm upset. Madison was..." She blinked slowly. After wiping her eyes, she lifted her chin. "We were friends."

"I'm terribly sorry for her loss," the king said, sincerity shining in his voice. He leaned forward, placing his elbows on his desk. "No one wants you to be happy here more than me. I facilitated this arrangement. You know my hopes, and they don't only include a treaty."

Rhaelyn crossed her arms over her chest. "I still want to leave."

"I see." His lungs expanded, then shot out his sigh. "I would never ask you to remain if you truly wish to leave. We can make arrangements for other women to take your place."

"Thank you," she said with quiet dignity.

"What about you, Nashio?" he asked.

"I want to leave too." Her voice broke, and she started to sob. Rhaelyn put her arm around the slender woman's shoulders. "I'm sorry, but I'm homesick already. Madison . . . and Crystal . . . It just makes me more eager to go home."

"I see," King Khaidill said. He pinched his eyes shut before opening them and directing them toward Betts. "And you?"

Her gaze shot to Nuvian before she leaned forward. "I'll stay."

Nuvian stared up at the ceiling, and I wondered what was going on between them. Wasn't Nuvian a lord and able to marry? It was clear Betts was interested in pursuing more, but he kept shrugging her off.

"And you?" the king asked me.

I glanced at Elion's stoic profile. He stared toward the bookcases behind the king so I couldn't read his thoughts.

But his fingers tightened around mine.

I thought of my sister waiting. She needed me. My cousin, who was doing all she could to be a substitute mom.

And of the bloody writing I'd seen on the wall.

My brain told me I'd be stupid to remain here to become the next victim. That I should return home and raise my sister. That nothing was going to come of this.

That I didn't need love.

As for my heart . . .?

I cleared my throat. "I'm staying."

Nuvian stood abruptly, making the chair he's sat in rock backward. It clattered on the floor, and the muted conversation in the room stilled.

With a growl, he launched himself across the table between us and smacked into me. Lifting me, he flung me over his shoulder.

He bolted from the room.

Chapter 24
Elion

With a roar, I took off after Nuvian, slamming across the room and through the door he kicked shut behind him. I barreled out into the hall, a snarl ripping up my throat.

Behind me in the green room, a clamor erupted, voices calling out in dismay. The king's bellow rose above them all. He wouldn't allow this insult to go unanswered. Nuvian would be lucky to get out of this with his skin.

But I'd get to him before the king. I would make him pay the price for his actions.

He was fast, but I'd wrestled and fought with him enough times while growing up to understand how he thought. He'd head for a place where he could complete his plan, and if I didn't catch up before that time, I'd never find him. He had always been loyal, but he was also clever.

The betrayal I felt from this was a fist in the gut. I

thought he could be trusted, even when everyone else shoved me aside.

Thankfully, Raven kicking and screaming on his shoulder slowed him down. I caught up to them before he reached the foyer, grabbing his arm and hauling him around to face me.

I reached for her but snapped my hands back when I saw the blade he held against her spine.

"Yes, back away," he said with a growl. His eyes glowed with rage, and florid color filled his cheeks. I hadn't seen him this angry since he learned his father killed his favorite pet. "Humans are such fragile creatures, don't you think? They're injured and die so easily."

"You killed the others?" Even as I said the words, I had a hard time believing them. Nuvian would go out of his way not to step on an insect. Murder just wasn't in him.

"There's always a first time," he said. He yanked Raven off his shoulder and tossed her down, her feet slamming against the floor.

She cried out. Before she could leap away, he shoved her against the wall, pinning her in place with a forearm, his knife pressed against her throat.

"Step away, Elion," he barked. "Unless you'd like a good view of her windpipe."

"I'll kill you for this," I growled, my wolf rising inside me. It begged me to release it, to let it rip him apart. He'd touched our mate, and now he would pay.

Enough, I told it in my mind, and it bared its teeth, a low rumble in its chest, but it obeyed me—for now.

"My death doesn't matter," Nuvian said. "As long as hers comes before mine."

"Why?" I asked. "We've been friends forever. You *were* like a brother to me." I stressed *were* in the statement. There would be no moving forward between us now.

His face cratered, telling me I'd struck a nerve. "I do this for you, Elion. For you." His hand trembled, the knife scraping Raven's delicate skin.

Her wide eyes met mine, and a tear traced down her cheek. Her fingers clenched and released, clenched and released at her sides. There wasn't anything she could do, and I hated that I couldn't end this immediately. I wanted to hold her and tell her everything would be all right.

Nothing would ever be the same.

One wrong move, and he'd kill her. I knew my friend well. He didn't make threats; he fulfilled every promise. That drew us closer. We'd both needed someone we could completely trust.

What about the promise he'd made to protect me? "She's a part of me. Without her, I'm nothing."

"You're the best, the reason I'm who I am," he said. His hand eased, and the blade stopped digging into her throat. "I hate having to do this, but I can't think of any other way to help you. Without her, you can fix this."

"There's no fix other than through her." I pressed my fist against my chest. "I know this. She is the key."

"There has to be another way."

"I don't want another way." I tried to reason with him. "I only want her."

Her gaze softened, and it struck me like lightning. She hadn't realized the depth of my feelings. Tears shimmered in her eyes, and I sensed they weren't from fear but from emotions brought to the surface by my words.

"It's not the way," Nuvian said with strengthening resolve. His hand tightened on the blade, and it dug against her skin again. "We'll handle this without her."

Fear wrenched my guts sideways. "Let her go."

"You can't be with her," Nuvian said. "She'll bring about your death."

"Not if she can save me," I said, pleading. I'd lay down my life to protect her. There was nothing I wouldn't give to ensure she was safe.

"What makes you think this lowly female can make a difference?" Nuvian asked with a sneer. "She is nothing. Let her go, and we can find a way to break your curse."

Fury filled her eyes, and for a moment, I swore they flashed icy blue. What had the witch seen in Raven that I hadn't?

Fae males had been known to cross the veil and prey on lonely human females. Raven said she didn't know who her father was.

Could he be one of us or—

Behind me, someone gasped. A crowd of fae pushed close. They watched with dismay. Others quietly cheered Nuvian on.

It didn't matter if she was full human or fae or the daughter of a troll. She was Raven. Perfection.

The only female I'd ever love.

"*She* told me Raven could make a difference," I said

in a low voice. There must be a way to get her out of his clutches. Once she was safe, I could pin him to the floor and make him see reason. Or kill him. At this point, he was beyond me; there was no repairing our friendship after this. "The witch knows who Raven is, and I believe she is not merely human."

"I don't believe it," he said, his gaze drifting away from her. "If it was true . . ." He shook his head, grabbing onto his resolve. "She's a puny human woman who can't even defend herself." He pressed his arm harder against her chest.

Raven gulped before stiffening. Something crossed her face . . . a mix of dismay and resolution.

Her gaze flashed to mine, and for a second, I swore I read her begging for forgiveness. She must know how torn I was about Nuvian.

Before I could figure out why she'd need my forgiveness, a feral snarl rose up her throat.

She ripped claws across his exposed forearm, filleting his skin.

Chapter 25
Raven

I stared down at my fingers, watching as claws magically oozed back into the tips, leaving my pink-painted nails behind.

It was only when I looked up that I realized fae aristocracy overfilled the foyer. Elion watched me with an impassive expression. Others pointed, whispering. Even the king stared at me with wide eyes.

What had just happened? I gaped at Elion while Nuvian reeled away, his face creased with pain.

He gulped. "What . . . ?"

"Seize him," King Khaidill growled, striding forward. He passed Elion, who still stared at my hand, and right up to me, putting his body between me and the others gathered in the room. "You have held something back from me, human."

The color suffusing his face told me how pissed off he was.

"I . . ." I shook my head. "I don't know what

happened." My gaze was yanked to the blood dripping off Nuvian's arm, splattering on the pretty marble floor. I inanely wondered who'd have to clean it up. "I didn't do it."

But I tore Nuvian's arm with claws I no longer possessed. How was that possible?

Elion strode around the king to take a place at my side. His arm went around my back, and he tugged me away from Nuvian. "Don't say anything," he whispered.

While I appreciated his support, I wasn't sure how we could keep this hidden. Everyone had seen. Did they understand what it meant? Because I didn't. It terrified me. Something had taken over and attacked. Nuvian deserved that and more, but how had I done it and what if whatever it was took control and went on a rampage?

The king waved his arm at his retainers. "Take Nuvian to the golden room. I will be there shortly to discuss his actions."

They barreled into him, slamming him against the wall, but he didn't fight them. He held out his hands, and they bound him with glistening magical bands before hustling him down the hall and through the door at the end.

"As for you, human," the king's glare hit me, "I will speak with you in the blue room as soon as I have taken care of this matter."

What would they do to Nuvian? I shouldn't care. He'd held a knife to my throat, and I was convinced he was going to kill me.

Trembles shook my body and my heart raced.

My world had just shattered, and I had no idea how to gather the pieces and glue them back together.

Elion's arm tightened around me, and his steady heartbeat sunk through my skin, grounding me. I leaned into him, wanting to cling.

My chest ached as multiple emotions poured through me. I couldn't sort through them, but I knew one thing. I was falling in love with Elion, and there was no way I could bring this to a halt.

Elion had declared himself for me. He cared. He wanted me in his life.

And he believed I could save him from the curse.

That thought wiggled through me like a worm through soft soil. How much of his caring was tied up in the idea I could end his curse? It was wrong of me to doubt him, but how could I do anything less? Everyone in the fae kingdom had an agenda, and none of their plans included ensuring I lived long enough to leave this place.

Elion had to be different.

It felt disloyal to believe anything else. He wasn't like them. He wouldn't do anything to hurt me. I knew this above everything else.

"I'm no savior," I said, needing him to know this. "I've been barely limping along since my mom died."

My sister. I hadn't thought about her for days. How could I fall for Elion when she needed me? Torn between the need to return to her and a longing to be with him, I wasn't sure what to think.

"Raven," Betts cried, rushing through the crowd to my side. She drew me into her arms, tugging me away from Elion. Her voice lowered, and she spoke for my ears alone. "Are you okay? Do you need to lay down?"

I mumbled something even I didn't understand. Chills wracked my frame, a reaction to what had just happened.

"How about a stiff drink?" she said.

My snort popped out, and I was grateful she was here with me. My hands shook, and maybe a shot of something strong would make them be still. "That might be good but—"

"The blue room," King Khaidill barked, his gaze taking in me and Elion. He pivoted on his heel and strode through the crowd with the rest of his entourage fluttering behind him. He growled at the others standing motionless, still gaping at me. "Find something to do. There's nothing more to see here."

"I'll go with you to the blue room," Betts said, her voice shining with loyalty.

"You will not," Elion said, though kindly. "The king will not speak with you present."

"We'll see about that," Betts huffed, though her shoulders curled forward. "What was Nuvian thinking?" Hurt came through in her words. "I liked him, and he tried to kill you."

He'd threatened me. Would he have killed me?

A shudder ripped through me. I didn't want to know the answer to that question.

I gave her a hug. "I'm sorry." There was no way I could explain his actions. I didn't understand myself.

"We need to go to the blue room," Elion said, ice glazing his eyes.

I sensed his anger wasn't directed at me. He must be horrified by how his best friend and advisor had behaved. Even terrified about the incident myself, I could understand how dismaying it would be if my best friend did something like that.

"I'll wait for you upstairs, then," Betts said, taking my hands and squeezing them. "We'll talk. The others plan to leave soon, and new women will arrive not long after. We need to come up with a plan."

For survival? Not a bad idea.

And I hadn't forgotten the message painted in blood on my bedroom wall.

I was next.

Chapter 26
Elion

We went to the blue room, which was a small receiving room on the back right side of the castle.

"I assume we'll need to stand," Raven said, nudging her hand toward the only chair in the room—a gilded bronze throne resting in the center of an equally gilded dais.

"You are correct," I said. My heart slammed hard against my ribs, and I struggled not to give way to my fear. I had no idea what the king would say to us, but I suspected it would not make us happy.

Raven strolled over to look out a window. "It's beautiful here. Everything is beyond perfect, like I've stepped into a fairytale or an amusement park."

"Amusement?" I asked, following her to the window. I'd follow her anywhere. Did she know this? My feelings were new and fragile—and unexpected. I'd never thought I'd have the chance to fall in love. And before I was cursed, I would've scoffed at the idea that I'd welcome such an emotion.

But I felt everything for Raven. She was the sun peeking above the horizon in the morning, plus the vast, churning sea full of intrigue and danger. Loving her was like stepping off a cliff and hoping I could fly.

Or that she'd catch me.

"Like Disney," she said. "Beautiful on the surface, but if you scrape away the gleam, you might find rot."

We would. "Not everything is horrible here."

She shot me a sad smile. "You're right. There are a few things worth admiring. And there's you."

"Raven," I breathed. I traced my finger down a strand of hair that had escaped her elaborate arrangement. I liked how it coiled around my finger, that it didn't want to let go, like it somehow reflected her feelings. It gleamed like trumknot wood sprites cut from a mythical tree that was said to grant wishes.

If I could have one wish, what would it be?

Her.

Even the chance to break the curse would be set aside if I could have this female in my life forever.

There was danger in thoughts like this. Nuvian wasn't the only one who would see my growing need. He wasn't the only one who'd try to take advantage of my feelings.

My love endangered her life.

In fact—

The door opened behind us, and the king strode

inside, his entourage with him. He waved them off, urging them to step back into the hall.

Only Nuvian remained with him when one of the guards pulled the door shut.

This suggested the king fully trusted me. Why else act as if he didn't need protection inside the blue room? His power was greater than mine, greater than almost anyone's throughout the kingdom, a gift granted to him by the spirits of his ancestors when he ascended to the throne.

Nuvian left the king and rushed across the room toward me and Raven.

I placed my body between him and her. She shrunk against the wall, though I noted her hands clenched into fists. She wouldn't let him get close enough to place a knife against her throat again.

Sadly, he wouldn't need to use his physical form to harm her; a flick of his finger, and he could magically choke her.

Not as long as I lived.

Nuvian dropped to his knees in front of me, bowing his head. "I apologize."

"You don't need to do so with me." I wasn't sure what I felt for him now. No one should ever have to choose between a good friend and love, because the wisest would always to follow their hearts. "Only Raven can forgive you, though I doubt she will."

She stepped up beside me and swallowed deeply. But before she could speak, her gaze followed the king as he strode to the dais and ascended to sit on his throne.

He watched us with sharp eyes, a hand settling on the arm of the throne with a finger lifted to deploy magic if needed. One wrong move on Nuvian's part, and his breath would cut off. The king never tolerated misbehavior.

"I apologize, *Raven*," Nuvian said, darting a sincere glance up at her before lowering his eyes. "I wanted to protect my friend, and I could see no other way of doing so other than by . . ."

"Killing me?" she said in a thready voice.

"I would not have harmed you."

"The knife to my throat suggested otherwise."

He pinched his eyes shut before opening them again. "I was going to take you back to your own realm. I planned to leave you there with enough coin to keep you happy for the rest of your days."

"What makes you think I'm here solely for money?" she asked, darting a look I couldn't decipher toward me.

He shrugged. "Aren't all of you here for that in one way or another?"

Her lips thinned and for a moment, I thought she wouldn't respond to his insult. "I will not deny that part of the lure. Just by coming here, I knew I would receive a settlement if I didn't choose to stay and marry." She turned pleading eyes my way. "My mother . . . She died, and there's so much debt. And I raise my little sister . . ." Her chest heaved with a sigh. "Things have changed since I arrived. I want something more precious than money, and I'm not afraid to say that."

Nuvian nodded slowly. "I understand. I see now

what I didn't before." His gaze spanned both of us, and there was no denying the pain I found on his face. It caught in my lungs, making it hard to suck in air.

We'd been friends—brothers—from the moment we met at three. It would be torture to thrust him from my life forever. But that decision needed to be made by Raven, and perhaps now was not the right time. We had so much to settle before we could talk about something like that.

"I will make reparations," Nuvian said, breaking the silence. He rose to his feet, shooting a glance at the king, who continued to watch benignly. "I will return to your ice-covered estate and do all I can to bring about a thaw."

That wasn't possible, but he was welcome to try if he felt that gave him a chance to make amends. My estate would not warm again until the moment I'd died of this curse.

"I will not return until I have completed this task," Nuvian said. His gaze flew to the king before returning to take in me, with Raven leaning against my side. "Again, I am sorry." With a dip of his head, he pivoted. He hurried from the room, and the door closed softly behind him.

"Come closer," King Khaidill told us. "I don't wish to yell when I speak with you both."

I took Raven's hand, and we walked over to stand a few feet in front of the dais.

The king did not miss that I kept hold of Raven's hand.

A snap of his fingers, and a chalice appeared,

followed by a bottle that poured dark blue liquid into the cup mid-air.

When the chalice nearly overflowed, the king blinked, and the bottle disappeared. He took the cup from the air and sipped the blue liquid.

Ermist, a rare and highly treasured wine. The grapes were said to only grow on the east side of the Vestibar Mountains. That blind sprites harvested the ripest of the grapes. That only one hundred bottles were crafted each season.

Of course, the king would have more than a season's worth in one of his wine cellars. It was one of his favorites.

"You need to leave the kingdom," the king said, and at first, I thought he meant Raven.

I stiffened when I noted his gaze resting solely on me.

"What do you mean?" I asked to give myself time to think.

"You understood my command," he said, his words echoed by Raven's gasp. "Leave the castle. Return to your estate. Do not go near this female again."

Chapter 27
Raven

"As long as you remain here, she will not seek another," the king snarled. "She only sees you."

"I have not cast a spell on her," Elion said sharply.

The king's intent gaze met his. "I never suggested you did."

I growled and took a step forward. "I will not seek anyone el—"

Elion laid a hand on my arm, holding back my words. I sensed he wanted me to remain silent, but how could I? This was my future the king had decided to play with.

"I should be among the choices," Elion said.

I'd heard no one dared argue with the king, and it crushed me that he'd risk everything to remain here.

"Don't you see?" Elion said. "She is my heart. My life. My future. I *crave* her."

My throat was tight with emotion, and I could barely breathe.

"You are cursed," the king said. "If you do not leave, I will add another curse to the first."

Would he really do that? How horrifying. I was right in my assessment of this place. Beauty on the surface, complete rot beneath.

Elion was the only light in this darkness.

"I do not wish to leave," Elion said. His words came out sharp, but a thread of desperation came through in his voice. "I *cannot*."

The king stared down his nose at Elion long enough I could barely keep from fidgeting. This was a reason he was king. He would make even a three-headed, mountain-sized Cerberus tremble.

"This is not open to debate," the king finally said.

"She is fated for me." Elion pressed a fist against his chest. "I know this."

"I don't want him to leave," I said, stepping forward. I kept my voice low and respectful. "Elion and I—"

"You are here to marry a lord," the king gritted out to me. "You are here to solidify our truce."

"Elion *is* a lord." Not that he'd proposed marriage or anything like that. I wasn't sure where our relationship was headed, but his words . . . They'd cracked my chest wide open.

If he got down on one knee and begged me to be his, could I deny him?

"He is cursed," the king said, smiling as if he hoped I'd gasp in horror or cringe away from the guy I was . . .

The guy I was falling in love with. Did I love him enough to fight for him?

My spine stiffened. "Even if his curse only gave me one minute with him, it would be worth it."

Elion watched me, a smile flitting across his lips. "Do you mean that?"

I nodded, then spoke in case that wasn't good enough. "I do."

"I will not argue about this any further," the king said. "As for what happened in the foyer . . ." His gaze dropped to my fingers.

Even now, I couldn't believe I'd sprouted claws. How was it possible?

Elion's finger flicked toward the king. "You saw nothing."

"I saw nothing," the king said in a dull voice.

Was he . . . casting a spell on the king to make him forget?

A door behind the throne swung inward, and the king's son and heir, Aillun, stepped through the opening.

The king shivered a second before stiffening. He watched as Aillun strode up onto the dais and joined him, standing at his left. Aillun's black, hawklike stare took in me, still holding Elion's hand, and his lips curled in a sneer.

He'd propositioned Betts. He'd watched us from the front deck when we first arrived. He was an absolute asshole. Pray the king outlived his son.

The king sipped his wine, and Aillun's gaze drifted to the glass. He watched as the king swallowed and lowered the glass onto a table on the right side of the throne.

The king's gaze briefly cutting to his son. "I was just

saying that there are plenty of lords for Raven to choose from in the fae kingdom. Don't you agree, Aillun?"

"Indeed, there are," Aillun said, giving his father a brief bow. "Many lords vie for her attention." His glare fell on Elion. "Since she is remaining here in the kingdom, she should choose one of them soon or leave."

"Why don't you select a few and make introductions?" The king's glare swept my way. "You will pick someone before the week is through and marry quickly after that."

I stepped forward. "I won't—"

A soft shuffling sound echoed behind us, and I shot a glance over my shoulder, my eyes widening when I took in a column of dark blue mist forming, like the ceiling and floor were forming a tornado. It's band whipped back and forth, partly coalescing into the shape of a person before turning back to mist.

"Be gone, Maverna" the king cried, standing. His hand lifted, his finger pointing in that direction. "You have no place here."

A cackle rang out. "You cannot command me, *King* Khaidill. I rule the forest. I will rule this kingdom as well, if I please."

I recognized the crotchety voice from the forest—the witch!

"I will leave soon," she said in a singsong voice. "For now, I am here to deal with them, not you." Her knobby hand swept toward us, and a thick band of slime erupted from the floor, oozing toward us.

Elion stepped between me and the sickly yellow

mass, whispering something in a language I didn't understand. The slime fizzled and thinned before being sucked into the cracks between the marble tiles.

The witch growled.

Elion lifted his arms and shot thin blades of white-blue lightning toward her. She ducked and released a shriek that was so high and intense it hurt. I slapped my hands over my ears.

"Begone," the king bellowed. Deep red flames burst past us like a gale force wind, billowing our clothing forward.

"Do not think you can play with me," the witch cried. Before the flames hit her, a pop rang out, and she started spinning, merging with the mist. The tunnel of mist split in the center. It was sucked up into the ceiling and down into the floor, leaving only the taint of mold lingering in the air.

Elion pulled me into his arms, and I pressed my face against his chest, breathing fast, like I'd run a race.

A gurgling sound made me look at the king.

He clutched his throat, his face flaring redder than the flames he'd just shot at the witch. His arm snapped sideways, hitting his wine glass and toppling it over. Deep blue liquid splattered onto the floor. It smoldered.

"Father," Aillun cried out in horror, grabbing the king's arm.

The king wrenched forward, out of Aillun's grasp. His finger pointed at Elion. "You . . . You . . ." With a hoarse cry, he toppled forward, smacking onto the marble floor.

ICE LORD'S BRIDE

He didn't move after that.

Chapter 28
Elion

"Arrest him," Aillun cried, pointing at me as the king's guards stormed into the room. "He murdered the king!"

Raven rushed to the king and stooped down beside him, laying a finger along his throat.

Aillun's quick spell hit me, wrapping invisible bands around my legs and arms. A flick of my finger broke the bonds, and a snarl ripped up my throat, making the others freeze and turn wide eyes my way.

"Do not do that again," I bit out.

"You murderer," Aillun bellowed. "I, as the new king, have every right to control my subjects."

"He isn't dead," Raven yelled over the voices calling out in dismay. She grabbed the king's shoulders and shook him before peering up at me. "He's breathing, but he's not responding."

"Arrest Elion," Aillun shouted. "He poisoned the king." He waved his hand to the ermist staining the pale marble floor and the glass lying next to it. "The evidence is there for all to see. Test it. You will find the spell and trace it back to Elion."

"He poured his own wine," Raven said. "He made a bottle appear from the air."

"Everyone knows of Elion's skills with magic," Aillun said. "They rival the king's!"

That was generous. No one's skills rivaled the kings . . . except Maverna's.

"It would be simple for him to add something to the liquid when my father wasn't looking," Aillun said.

"The same could be said for you, Aillun," I said dryly, stepping closer to Raven to protect her. There was no saying what Aillun would do with her now. He opposed the human-fae marriage plan. Rumor had it he wasn't upset a few had died.

"How dare you accuse me?" Aillun sputtered.

I grunted, well aware of where he was taking this. "I dare as much as you."

I regularly protested his restrictive actions here in the kingdom. He'd promised revenge for this in the past. Whatever happened to the king in my presence had handed an opportunity to him.

"I assure you; I didn't do anything to his wine," I told the guards gathering around me, infusing a truth spell into my words. The glow around me would prove I was being honest.

"See the aura?" one said, pointing. "He didn't harm the king."

Uncertain, the others shuffled their feet and exchanged heavy glances.

"The witch did this," Raven said. "She was here, and she made threats."

Maverna not only threatened the king; she'd threatened me and Raven. My powers were not great enough to keep her away.

Raven carefully rolled the king over onto his back. His tongue lolled, poking out of his mouth, and he gurgled again. "Get a healer here immediately. There must be someone who can help him."

The urgency in her voice transmitted itself to the others, giving them something to do other than struggle to avoid obeying Aillun's command to arrest me.

They must hope the king would waken and take charge again, relieving Aillun of the role he was all too eager to step into.

He may be the heir to the throne, but he couldn't seize control like this. It still needed to be handed to him, along with the boost of magic only the king of our land commanded.

One of the guards mumbled an incantation.

A healer appeared at the doorway within seconds, others crowding behind her. She cried out when she saw the king lying still on the floor and rushed into the room.

Raven rose and backed into the shelter of my arms while the healers encircled the king.

They held hands and swayed, reciting a spell in the ancient language only a few now understood.

"He is ensorcered," one wailed. "Ensorcered!" She

flicked her hand to the cup and stain on the floor, and they disappeared, spirited to the healer's chambers.

Even without my truth aura, my magical abilities did not extend to something like this, a fact Aillun would be well aware of.

He may wish to lock me up, but it was clear the guards weren't comfortable with the plan.

"We will save him," a healer cried.

"Save him," the others echoed.

"Please," Aillun said, his face a mesh of pain. "Help my father."

The king's image wavered, as did the healer's, until they all disappeared. They'd take him to his suite and work magic to diagnose the spell. Then they'd find a way to reverse it.

"The witch was here," Raven continued. "She threatened the king. She did this, not Lord Elion."

The king's guards looked from Aillun to me. It was clear they weren't sure what to do. With the king unconscious and possibly dying, there was no one to give orders.

Those who deferred to Aillun now would have favor if the king did not recover. Those who disobeyed could find themselves expelled from the kingdom.

One of them bowed to the prince, and the others soon followed. The king was unconscious. Someone must rule, and it was appropriate for Aillun to step into that role for now.

My heart sunk. I'd shown I was innocent, but it was clear they'd chosen sides already. Curse Nuvian for betraying me. I needed him here to watch my back.

"What would you have us do, your highness?" the head of the king's detail asked, shooting a look of sympathy my way. Obeying a ruler they loved was one thing. Obeying someone they'd despised—though they kept it well hidden—was another.

Aillun nodded benignly, keeping his sharp gaze pinned on me. A smile fluttered across his lips, and I could tell he enjoyed this new role already.

The mantle of power had never fit well on his shoulders.

"Allow me to think a moment," he said. He turned and leisurely climbed onto the dais, where he took his father's place on the throne. His attention drifted across Raven, and for one moment, I spied lust.

I tightened my arms around her. She wasn't safe here and not only from Maverna.

If I was wise, I'd ignore my heart—ignore my determination to break the curse. And if I was even wiser, I'd pretend Raven meant nothing to me.

My guts wrenched sideways. I couldn't push her away. Like I'd told the king, I *craved* her. Was there any way around this?

A growl ripped through me.

Tightening my arms around her, I leaned forward and lowered my voice for her ears alone. "I'm sorry, Raven. I'm sending you back to the human realm immediately."

Chapter 29
Raven

Dismay dropped onto me like a heavy weight. I tugged against Elion's grasp, but he held me in the shelter of his arms.

Shelter? No, he was sending me away.

"I won't go," I hissed.

"It's the only way to keep you safe," he whispered.

"You think whatever's hunting me here won't follow?"

We spoke low, but that didn't mean no one heard. The guards watched us intently, speculation on their faces, and an irritating smile kept twitching the corners of Aillun's mouth upward.

"I will protect you," he said.

I looked up at him. "Does that mean you're coming with me?"

He sighed. "I cannot."

"Then I'm not going anywhere. If you're going to protect me, do so here." Frankly, there were a few tricks I could deploy to protect myself. I wasn't a Boston girl for nothing.

"As for you two," Aillun said. "My father made his wishes quite clear, and I will follow through with his command. Before the week is through, Raven, you will pick someone and marry thereafter."

"You can't make me do it," I said, pulling out of Elion's embrace and putting a step between us. I needed to think, and I couldn't do it when he was touching me. "When we came here, we were told we could choose, and if we didn't find someone we wanted to marry, we could leave." I didn't even care about the money they'd offered those who left. I wanted my chance to pick my own future restored. "You can't change the rules and say I now only have days to decide."

"I can do whatever I wish," he said with a sneer. "But in this, I follow my father's decision. The others are leaving today. New women will arrive soon, and I will ensure the timeframe is tighter this time."

"But the treaty—"

"Doesn't specifically name how long the women have to choose. They will pick quickly, or I will pick for them." His evil smile rose. "You as well. I'm sure there are plenty of lords, or even royalty itself, who would be willing to take you to their bed."

Royalty. Did he mean himself? A shudder ripped through me.

"*They will marry by choice*, not be taken to a bed without consent," Elion growled. "I will not permit this. Nor will the other lords."

Fear flashed across Aillun's face, quickly replaced by anger. "Do not speak to the lords about this."

Did they have some say in this? The king appeared all powerful—and now his son had taken his place—but maybe if the lords got together, they could keep this travesty from occurring.

Aillun shoved down a swallow, and shrugged. "If it solidifies the truce, most are willing to go through a human ceremony. You know it means nothing here."

"What does that mean?" I asked, looking between them.

"The fae don't marry like humans do," Elion said.

"Exactly," Aillun said. "We have sex with whoever we choose. An heir can then be selected from among many." He leaned forward and clapped his hands. "Take Raven to her room. She has decided to remain here within the fae kingdom and is thus subject to my rules. See that she does not . . . wander."

I bolted for the open window, determined to leap out and run, but a couple of the guards surrounded me quickly and pinned my arms behind my back. When I kicked and tried to bite them, one cast a spell over me, locking my arms to my sides and my ankles together. A scream burst from me, but it was cut off by magic as well.

"Raven," Elion bellowed, rushing toward me. The rest of the guards used magic to bring him to a standstill while Aillun watched, a slick grin on his face.

Magic crackled across the tips of Elion's fingers. The guards lifted their hands toward him, and Elion's magic extinguished. There were too many of them for him to overcome.

The guards carried me out into the hall. Tears fell from my eyes, the only part of my body I could control.

The remaining guards dragged Elion from the room. Where would they take him?

I realized Aillun had not been in the room when the king questioned me about the claws I still couldn't believe I'd used on Nuvian. Could this be my advantage?

A glance at the grim-faced guards suggested caution. If they could overcome Elion so easily, as they should be able to do since they protected the king, they could easily handle me wielding claws. Assuming I could make them appear again.

Aillun also hadn't been there when the king told Elion to leave the kingdom. Unless he'd been listening in the hallway outside the blue room. He hadn't brought it up, so there was still hope Elion would be allowed to remain nearby. If they didn't lock him up, we stood a chance of making this right, though I had no idea how we'd do it.

As the guards started carrying me up the stairs, Elion's call rang out behind us. "Trust me, Raven. I will come for you!"

I wanted to reply, but all I could choke out was a strangled gurgle.

Fury blasted through me. I hated losing control of my life and my body. I'd make Aillun pay.

They deposited me in the room, and I remained in place, bound while they left, locking the door behind them. Only then did the magic release. I flexed my arms and shifted my legs until I felt confident no magic lingered to slow me down.

I ran to the window. When I touched it, a shock jolted up my arms to my chest. I gasped and took a step backward.

I'd already determined there was no way out from the bathroom. They'd blocked all escape.

For now.

I glared down at my hands, trying to will them to form claws. Then I could rip my way through the wall and find Elion. But no matter how hard I wanted, I couldn't make it happen. Had I imagined it? No, I hadn't imagined the cuts on Nuvian's arm or his blood dripping from the wounds.

Movement below caught my eye, and I carefully approached the window to look out.

Betts ran toward the woods. Go, I wanted to shout, but I didn't want to call anyone's attention. Was she fleeing? Good for her.

Someone stepped out of the woods, and for a second, I worried the cloaked figure could have bad intentions. Until the hood fell back on his shoulders, revealing Nuvian.

She stopped in front of him, and they spoke heatedly. He kept shaking his head, flinging his arm toward the castle. She stomped her foot and crossed her arms over her chest.

Finally, his back tightened, and even from the distance, I could read his glare of frustration.

Then he held his hand out to her.

She tightened her grip on the bag looped over her shoulder and took his hand.

As they hurried into the woods together, she looked back.

I swore her solemn gaze met mine before she was swallowed by the darkness.

Chapter 30
Elion

I should be grateful I was only locked in my rooms and not chained to a wall in the dungeon. I wasn't worried about myself. Raven was my sole concern.

I'd declared myself for her and her for me, but would we be allowed to act on our feelings?

Within days, she'd be forced to choose someone to marry. On top of that, the king had told me I must leave. I was grateful he was unconscious and thus couldn't enforce his order. He was a friend. But I was grateful Aillun had not overheard all the king's words. If only he hadn't heard the command that Raven marry.

I paced my room half the night, periodically testing the magical bonds placed on my doors and windows. They'd been crafted by masters, but that epitomized the king's guard. He kept only the best within his inner circle.

Finally, I slept.

Only to be woken in the morning when Follen crept

into the room. He opened the drapes, allowing dawn to cut through the glass.

"Have you heard anything about the king?" I asked.

His tight gaze traveled across my face before his posture loosened. "He is unresponsive, but he still lives. There are rumors . . ."

"That I'm involved."

"No one could convince me you would do something like that, sir," he said, the high color in his pointed ears showing he was clearly affronted.

"I was in the room when it happened, as was the human woman, Raven."

"I've heard Maverna could be involved."

"She threatened the king in my presence."

"Then it's clear she did something to harm our king. We can't stand for this." He lifted the shirt I'd tossed onto a chair the night before and held it out. A blink of magic, and it was clean again. Turning, he approached the closet to hang it with the others.

"You're right," I said. "We need to punish whoever did this to our sovereign. She was not the only person with us in the room, however."

Follen came to a halt, though he didn't turn my way. "Who else was there?"

"Aillun," I said softly. It could be a mistake adding the prince's name to the list of suspects, but I'd be wrong to withhold this information.

Many would be happy if the king never woke, including his son.

"Ah, I see," Follen said, carefully hanging my shirt in the closet. "I will hold this information close."

As always, I could trust this elf with anything, including my life.

"Shall I draw you a bath, sir?" he asked, his voice brighter. He'd file away the details for now, but it wouldn't be long before he'd shared them with a few select elf staff. They may hide things from us, but they rarely did so with each other. "I will also obtain a tray from the kitchens for breakfast."

"Yes to the bath, but I will dine downstairs." Nothing would keep me from Raven. We needed to speak where no one could overhear. We needed to plan, though I wasn't sure there was much we could do.

My curse meant nothing when compared to the thought of losing her. Yes, my life would end within a year, but what was living if she couldn't share the time with me? Knowing this solidified my resolve. We'd find a way to get out of this trap.

"Very well, sir," Follen said. A snap of his fingers, and the large tub appeared near a window, followed by the slosh of water.

I rose and strode into the bathroom, returning to the room and removing the scrap of cloth I wore at night only to keep my elf friend from gasping in dismay. Elves considered modesty as one of their primary virtues, going so far as to wearing scraps of fabric even when they bathed. We'd compromised with me wearing something when he was around, *other* than when I sunk into the tub.

He pivoted sharply as I untied the groin covering and tossed it aside.

I stepped into the tub and sat, moving down into the water until only my head remained uncovered.

"I will lay out clothing," Follen said.

"Thank you."

He obtained a shirt and pants from the closet and laid them on the bed.

"The door . . ." I grabbed a bar of soap and started washing.

"What about it?"

"It was unlocked when you arrived."

He stiffened. "No, sir. Not at all. It was locked, as usual."

"As usual?"

"I was only able to open it because of the charm you gave me."

Charm . . .Yes. Now that was an idea.

"As always," Follen said, "the charm allowed me past the magical barriers you erected when you first moved into the castle."

I'd set them so long ago, I'd almost forgotten. "No other magic held you back?"

He frowned. "What other magic could there be?"

There was no need to keep this hidden; he'd hear about what happened from the other staff soon. I was surprised he hadn't already. "Aillun sent me to my rooms last evening under guard." A polite way of phrasing their actions. "I assumed they'd added magical barriers to the door when it wouldn't open."

"They locked you in?" he gasped, his spine stiffening. "How dare they? I will—"

"Take care," I said. "With the king unable to resume command, anything is possible."

He dipped forward in a brief bow. "Wise advice. We must all take care until the king awakens."

I appreciated his loyalty, but I refused to let him do something that would turn Aillun's wrath in his direction. As long as word spread to those who needed to be in the know, I was satisfied.

He sniffed. "I am surprised even the king's guard would dare cast a spell to keep you inside your rooms."

"You have more confidence in my abilities than me." I sunk down beneath the water to wet my hair and started lathering it. "You'll let me know if you hear anything vital?" He could be trusted to be discrete when he asked questions.

"Of course." He strode to the door while I rubbed my scalp, savoring the comfort I took from the simple gesture. "Can I do anything else for you, sir?"

"Could you ask Erleene to come to my rooms shortly? I need something from her."

"Are you sure?"

Erleene was the most powerful elf wizard in his clan, though few sought her services due to her price since very few could afford to pay. Crossed, she would exact a revenge that could rival the curse Maverna placed on me.

I'd gone to Erleene before Maverna's curse had fully set, but by then, it was too late. Erleene told me breaking it would break *her*. She'd apologized, stating plainly she couldn't take on Maverna's wrath, not even for me, someone she mostly considered a friend.

Mostly. Was there anyone she'd sacrifice herself for in this world?

"I'll be careful," I said.

"As always, I will defer to your judgment." Follen's frowning gaze drifted around the room as if seeking something he could do other than this, but he'd tidied already. His sigh rang out. "And I will ask a sprite to take a message to Erleene."

A sprite would be quickest. If I knew Follen, Erleene would arrive here before I'd finished dressing.

Once Follen left, I finished rinsing and rose from the tub. I dried and dressed quickly. A sweep of my hand, and the tub and water disappeared. The water would automatically be dumped into the moat, and the tub would remain in the ether world until it was needed once more.

I was buttoning up my shirt when Erleene appeared. As she approached me, her dark cloak swept across the floor, her bare feet poking from beneath. She'd pinned her white hair streaked with green up onto her head, pulling it tight enough to stretch her lineless cheekbones.

"You have need of me, Ice Lord?" she asked, bowing forward while keeping her gaze trained on mine. She sought answers I wasn't going to give.

I scoffed; confident I was better at hiding than she believed.

Her title of Ice Lord wasn't an insult. I and my favorite estate had been encased in ice after Maverna cast her spell. I'd broken through some of the magic holding me entombed, enough to free myself to this minimal existence, but I'd been unable to break her spell further. What Nuvian thought he could do that I couldn't was beyond me.

I quickly explained what I needed from Erleene.

"Who is this young lady?" she asked, a sly smile rising on her face, making her look decades younger than she truly was. As far as I knew, few knew much about this elf, which was the way she liked it. If she maintained a cloak of mystery, people feared her and kept their distance.

Unless they were desperate like me.

"She's someone I wish to help," was all I was willing to say.

"I see." Her pert nod told me she respected me for withholding information. Frankly, as long as I was willing to pay her steep price, she would defer asking questions.

I held out my hand, and she tapped it, extracting the price needed.

Sucking in a deep breath, I struggled not to stagger.

"You charge too much," I snarled.

"Not for something such as this." Her hand lifted. "Do you want the energy back, or do you still wish for the contracted magic? Decide now."

"I want it." Truly, there was no price I wouldn't pay.

"Very well," she said, rewarding me with a sharp smile. "I will be delighted to oblige the Ice Lord in this task."

Chapter 31
Raven

I woke to a heavy weight dropping onto my chest. My eyes popped open, then widened as I took the horrifying sight.

A misty, four-legged creature about the size of a hyena stood on my chest. As I gulped and bucked, trying to dislodge it, it opened its jaws, revealing fangs the length of my thumbs.

Dingy blue smoke shot from its lungs and hit my face. It coiled down to encircle my throat, tightening until I couldn't breathe.

Bitter shrieks erupted from inside me, and I wrenched myself from side to side on the bed, but the creature held on, smoke still pouring from its lungs to strangle me.

You're next. The words written on my wall in Madison's blood flashed through my mind. I hadn't forgotten, but I'd naively believed I was safe inside a locked room—

something I would be at home but never in a world filled with magic.

Filled with evil magic.

Tiny stars tumbled around me as my brain began to succumb to the lack of oxygen. My whimpers were caught in the back of my throat.

My heart floundering, I grunted, flailing my arms and legs, but my strength was leaving me, drained away by this magical creature. I had no control over my fate. It would hold on until I stopped moving. They'd find me dead, and if I was like the others, they'd call it an accident or natural causes.

By the time anyone arrived, the creature would've fled, leaving behind marks on my neck that would fade before anyone saw them.

This thing had killed the other women. It had come for me, and there was no escaping its clutches.

I flailed, hitting out, but my hands passed through it. How could I get free if I couldn't get it off me?

My mind blurred, and I struggled to hold on. I wasn't ready to go. I had so much to live for. My little sister loved me.

Elion.

No, no. Please.

My head thrashed on the bed, and tears leaked from the corners of my eyes. My lungs burned and gasped for air.

My door opened and the pretty elf who drew my bathwater and brought me snacks stepped inside, holding a dress she must be planning to suggest I wear today in one arm and Koko, my fluffy resha, cradled in the other.

Poor Koko was about to see me die. As for the dress, I wouldn't be wearing it anywhere except for my upcoming funeral.

She stopped in the middle of the room, her jaw dropping. The dress slipped from her hand, fluttering to the floor like a ghostly apparition. Holding Koko close, she turned and raced from the room. She'd go for help, but it was already too late.

No.

Anger rose within me, shoving aside the overwhelming urge to give up. I wasn't going to do it. I would not allow a mist hyena to kill me.

This was what murdered the other women. I knew it.

I drew on something buried deep inside me, a part of myself I'd never set free. I wasn't magical, but that didn't mean I didn't have power. It lurked within me, and it had manifested itself when Nuvian held the knife to my throat.

The skin on my neck burned as the hyena tightened its smoky hold. Its claws dug into my chest. A feral look filled its eyes, and I swore I also read glee there. It savored watching me die.

I had to turn the tables. I must destroy it.

I pinched my eyes shut and willed it to happen.

Claws jutted out from my fingers, long and sharp. They were mine, and I belonged to whatever gave them to me. There was a part of me I needed to discover, explore, and unleash.

I struck out at the creature, expecting my claws to sink through it like my nails, but my claws impacted with something solid.

Latching onto its throat, I gave it a taste of what it was doing to me. As rage roared through me, I tightened my hold, my claws digging into the mist hyena's skin. I ripped, slicing deep enough to hit bone.

The creature tipped its head back and shrieked. Now it was the one struggling.

Yelping, it released my neck. I gulped in air, savoring the wonder of being able to breathe.

Bucking, I wrenched the creature sideways, pressing it onto the mattress. I shredded it while mist blood flew around us before dissipating in the air.

"Raven," someone cried, but I couldn't look away from the beast that had tried to kill me. No more would magic control me. Not when I could do this.

I ripped down its belly, cackling when its misty guts spilled out. It thought *it* was feral; it thought *it* was in control.

How dare it try to kill me?

"Raven." A hand landed on my shoulder, squeezing gently. "Stop. It's over. Release it."

"Elion?" I whimpered, coming back into myself, like I'd been dropped from a ten-story building and landed solidly on my feet on the pavement below, as safe as I'd been before I fell.

My claws loosened, releasing what was left of the mist creature. They retracted, sinking back into me as if they'd never been there. But now I felt them. They waited to strike again when I needed them. A promise between me and whatever lurked inside me.

"Raven," Elion said again, softly.

"I . . . I . . ." I rolled back off my knees, landing on the bed on my butt, lifting my hands up. I expected to find blood, but only my smooth skin met my gaze. I clawed at my aching throat, but I suspected the marks the beast inflicted were already fading. "I don't know what I did, but I'm glad it happened."

A pop resounded in the room, and everything making up the shredded beast exploded, its misty form blasting out before floating down to the floor like dust. The floorboards absorbed it, leaving nothing behind but the taint of brimstone and ash. Who would've thought I'd come to recognize the smell so easily?

Elion limped over and sat on the bed. He tugged me up onto his lap, holding me. His chin dropped to the top of my head.

"It's all right," he said. "You're safe."

"I am," I said in a voice stronger than I'd expect. I should be sobbing, terrorized by what just happened, but I wasn't. I felt as if I'd finally begun to come into my own power. "I did it. I killed the creature that murdered my friends."

Chapter 32
Elion

I waved for Maecia to come closer, but though she left the open doorway, she paused halfway toward the bed.

"Do not speak of this to anyone," I said.

"But sir . . ." Her wide eyes spiraled around the room. "Mistress Raven was nearly killed by a cinder. We must notify everyone in the kingdom."

"I will do so, but I ask you not to share this. The king . . ." I pinched my eyes shut before opening them again. Who knew what was going to happen to the king? Everything was unsettled. "Once he awakens, the king will know best how to handle this."

I knew how I planned to handle it. I'd protect Raven at all costs.

"The king is still unconscious?" Raven asked, easing off my lap. She stood, and while her hands trembled, her stiffening body told me fury was shoving aside her terror of what had just happened.

"Unfortunately, yes."

"Which means Aillun's still in charge," she said, her shoulders sinking.

I nodded, not wishing to voice my feelings about his rule in front of Maecia, let alone with the door to the hall open.

"I'll notify him first thing," I said.

"Perhaps you are right," Maecia said. "It would frighten many who serve the kingdom to hear that one of . . . *her* minions could enter the castle this easily."

She meant Maverna, the witch who'd cursed me.

"What are we going to do, then? We can't leave this unanswered," Raven snarled.

Meeting Maecia's eyes, I lifted my chin, urging her to leave.

"I should prepare Mistress's bath first," she said. A wave of her hand and a tub holding steaming water appeared. Maecia lifted a dress from the floor, smoothed it, and laid it on the foot of the bed. "Will you be dining downstairs this morning, or would you prefer a tray after what happened?" she asked Raven.

I struggled not to gnash my teeth at her persisting in these normal tasks, but I didn't wish to frighten the elf. She'd be more willing to do as I asked if I held my tongue and didn't use it to lash her.

"I'll . . ." Raven's gaze met mine, and I assumed she wasn't sure which was the best path to take.

"We will both eat downstairs," I said.

"All right," Raven said. "Thank you, Maecia. I appreciate all your help."

Maecia bowed and left the room, shutting the door behind her.

"I have something for you," I said, approaching Raven. I spirited the charm from the air where I'd hidden it from view, and held it out, the gold chain gleaming in the sunlight. Deep red beams spiraled off the precious jewel.

"What is it?" Raven breathed, holding her hand out toward the charm before snatching it back.

"It's for you," I said. "Turn, and I'll help you secure it around your neck."

She pivoted, and I moved in close behind her, magically fusing the charm around her neck.

"I ask you not to remove it," I said.

"You gave it to me. I have no wish to take it off again." She gasped when she smoothed a finger across the stone. "It's warm. Is that because you held it against your skin?"

"It warms for you." Like I did. Like I always would.

The soft smile she released as she gazed down at it dangling between her breasts made my heart surge up in my throat. To think I'd come close to losing her.

Breaking my curse meant nothing if I couldn't have Raven beside me always.

"It's gorgeous," she said.

Erleene had mounted the thumbnail sized stone in a gold setting to match the chain.

"It will protect you," I said.

"In what way?" She continued to admire it.

"It will block most spells."

"No one will be able to force me to do something I don't want to? I like that idea."

"It won't stop all magic, but most will be absorbed by the stone. When it blocks something malicious, you'll feel it tingle. It'll warm when I'm near because it will feed off my magic. If nothing else, it'll alert you when someone tries to control you."

Her fingers stilled. "Will it stop a cinder?"

"Yes."

"Thank you."

"You can't trust it completely."

"That's why I have you," she said softly.

"You do have me. Always." Warmth crashed through me. To think she felt about me the way I did her. It stunned me. Humbled me. And made my heart race.

While she stroked the stone, I drank in the scent of her hair and the warmth of her body. Heat burst through me, reminding me all over again of how much I wanted this woman, how I'd do anything to be with her.

Somehow, I could bear having Maverna hate me, though I had no idea why she did. But the thought of her taking her anger out on Raven, the most precious person in my life, made rage crash through me. It was a driving force that would not stop until I'd ravaged the world.

There was no telling what I'd do to Maverna if she was here right now.

Raven wore almost nothing, just a short gown that barely skimmed the tops of her thighs. It plunged down to reveal the mounds of her breasts, and all I could think of was how wonderful it was when she fell apart in my arms that night in the garden.

It might be greedy, but I wanted to feel that again.

I shifted her glorious hair to the side and, because I couldn't resist, kissed from behind her ear down her neck.

She melted back against me. "Elion." My name came from her lips in a sigh full of need. "You're very distracting."

"Do you wish to be distracted?"

Her low laugh rang out. "I should be freaking out right now. A magical creature just tried to kill me, but I fought it off and possibly killed it. I think. Now to hear the witch sent it after me makes my knees quake."

"I was hoping I was making your knees quake."

"You do." She turned and placed her sweet hands on my shoulders. "I need you. Is that a bad thing to say?"

My groan slipped out. "There's nothing bad if it involves us."

"You say the most amazing things." A smile flirted across her lips. "The total opposite of how you spoke when we met up here at the castle the first time."

"I was stunned by your beauty and how much I wanted you."

"I'll forgive you for being snarly, then." Her full smile bloomed.

I couldn't do anything less than tug her closer and kiss her. Remembering how close I'd come to losing her made the bonds I'd secured around my control let go. My tongue plundered her mouth.

Moaning, she pressed herself against me.

I backed her against the wall and bunched up the hem of her thin gown.

When she spread her thighs to welcome my touch, I pulled down her panties.

"Yes," she sighed against my skin when my fingers found her wet warmth. She dripped for me, and there was nothing I wanted more than to bury my cock deep inside her. The thought of her writhing beneath me, moaning as she came from my touch, unleashed something feral inside me.

Part of me *was* a beast. I'd blocked it off deep inside, only releasing the wolf when I had great need. But the driving need I sensed in the creature matched mine.

"Raven," I growled.

She spread her legs wider, her head tipping backward against the wall. Her eyelids closed, and she breathed as if she'd run forever.

I glided a finger inside her and groaned at how slick she was. My thumb found her clit while I moved two fingers within her. When I rubbed her clit, she arched toward me, gasping with joy.

I lifted her, and her legs went around me.

"Mine," I growled. "You are all mine."

"Yes," she cried, bucking against my fingers pushing inside her. "I'm going to . . ."

"Take it," I said against her neck. Her skin held the sheen of desire, and I licked it, savoring the salty flavor of lust and need.

"Take me, Elion. Please." She slammed her hips

forward, straining to push my fingers deep inside. "I need you."

There was nothing I wanted more.

I grappled with the fastening on my pants. My cock was a thick rod, straining toward my abs. It would be so easy to bury myself inside her, to rock against her until she exploded from my touch.

Her eyes met mine. "I mean it, Elion. I want you. All of you. Everything."

"The prince—"

"Is not in this bedroom."

The thought that I could lose her made my inhibitions come undone. I'd die if I didn't have this moment to cling to. "I'll fight to claim you as my own, to make you mine forever," I said against her skin.

"And I'll fight for you." Her heady gaze met mine. "Nothing and no one is going to drive us apart."

"Nothing," I said, centering the head of my cock at her core. "No one."

I drove my cock deep within her core.

Chapter 33
Raven

We may not have planned to have sex, but damn, I wanted him. Everything and everywhere. It wasn't just the fact that we might be driven apart soon. Or that the witch could send another cinder after me.

I wanted Elion. I had from the moment I met him back at the diner.

There was no describing the feelings pouring through me as his gaze locked with mine and he started moving.

His cock was long and thick, and with each thrust, he hit deep within me, sending shock waves of pleasure to my soul. His body shifted against mine as he moved, rubbing against my clit in the best way possible.

I wanted this to last forever, but I was going to come in seconds.

He kissed me, and his tongue stroked mine, drawing out my passion. I slipped my hands beneath his shirt, desperate to feel his skin, desperate to touch him.

He held my butt in place with one hand, while his

other roamed my breasts, gently rolling the nipples. I was on fire, and only he could turn the feeling into a roaring blaze.

As my body started spiraling, he went faster, driving into me over and over, his hips nearly a blur. Our groans filled the room.

"Elion," I cried as my mind shot to the stars. His cock gliding within me and his body rubbing against mine made my world lose focus. Only Elion and his body mattered.

This wasn't about possession, though I felt fully claimed. And it wasn't about satisfying our body's needs.

Our two hearts were fusing together. Becoming one. I couldn't understand how I knew this, but I'd never experienced anything like this before. I felt like my heart reached out to his, and he not only cupped it in his warm palm, but he also held it tight with a determination to never let go.

I didn't think it could get better, but he increased his pace, driving into me faster. When his fingers found my clit and rubbed it, my eyes rolled back in my head. An orgasm roared through me, starting within my bones and making all of me quiver. I rode it while he rode me, gasping through one burst after another.

When he groaned and shot everything he had inside me, I came again, like his seed was a stimulant all by itself.

His head dropped, and he buried his face in my neck, breathing fast. "You are perfect. Precious. Amazing."

"You're not too bad yourself," I said with a grin,

rubbing his shoulders. I wanted to cling to him. Dance around the room to show him how happy I was. Drag him to the bed and do it again.

His cock twitched inside me. "Humans use protection."

Oh shit. "I'm not on the pill, and I don't have an implant."

"If a fae wishes to impregnate someone, an implant or pill will not stop them."

I cocked one eyebrow at him. "Are you saying you *want* to get me pregnant?"

"I cannot."

"You're shooting blanks?"

He frowned before a grin unlike anything I'd seen before split his face. He was devilishly handsome when he smiled. "I never do anything partway, and I never shoot . . . blanks."

Leave it to a guy to be cocky about his sperm count. "So why no protection?" I couldn't blame him; that had been the last thing on my mind when he lifted me, and I wrapped my legs around him. It never occurred to me to bring condoms to the fae kingdom. I hadn't planned on falling in love with Elion.

He stroked my face before stepping away from me and securing his pants, carefully tugging down my nightie. Kneeling in front of me, he kissed both my thighs, looking up at me with lust blooming again in his eyes.

He picked me up and strode to the bed, dropping down onto the surface, taking me with him. I nestled on his chest, watching his face.

"Fae and humans cannot share . . ." He frowned. "I am not sure of the term."

"STDs?"

His frown deepened.

"It means sexual diseases."

"Yes, that is the term." His expression cleared. "We do not use protection at all. We cannot sicken in that manner, and when a male wishes to impregnate someone, they force a chemical change within their body that transmits to their chosen one. Only then can that person ripen to receive seed."

Ripen. Like a piece of fruit. "Hold the ripening idea for now." While I was grateful that I couldn't catch a fae STD, a disconcerting thought occurred to me. "Are you saying you *don't* want to get me pregnant?" Two seconds ago, I was worried "ripening" things could be happening deep inside me already. Now I felt sad that the chance wasn't there.

He groaned and kissed me quickly. "Nothing would make me happier than to see you carrying my child, but it is too dangerous now."

"You're talking about the curse."

"That and the situation with the king."

"If I was pregnant, would he force me to marry you?"

"It would be a blessing to claim you as my bride," he said, his sincere gaze meeting mine. "There would be no force needed. I want you desperately. But I worry that—"

My door banged open, and the king's guard stormed inside, their arms lifting and magic arcing across their fingers.

They rushed to the bed and ripped me from Elion's arms, tossing me toward the wall. Hitting hard, I cried out and lunged away from the surface, trying to get past them to reach Elion.

"Raven." Elion snarled and shot lightning at the guards, but they deflected it. They bound him with magic, hauled him from the bed, and dragged him out the door.

I raced after them.

Aillun waited in the hall, his face scarlet with fury.

"What are you doing?" Elion bellowed, struggling to break free. "Release me."

"You are under arrest," one of the guards said.

"For what?" Elion asked, scowling at Aillun.

Aillun's lips twitched upward before smoothing, replaced by another flash of anger. "The king has died. You murdered my father!"

His arm lifted, and he magically flung Elion against the wall.

Elion's head hit hard, his head slamming against the surface.

He slid to the floor, unconscious.

Chapter 34
Elion

I woke lying on my bed, and for a moment, I wasn't sure where I was. Had I dreamed of loving Raven, and then Aillun calling for my arrest for the murder of the king? The pounding in the back of my head proved everything had happened.

A flick of my hand, and my headache eased. I was no healer, but I could apply simple pain relief spells to myself.

The magical bonds the guards applied had faded. I leaped from my bed and stalked to the door, finding it locked. This was no surprise.

I blasted magic at it a number of times, but though the knob heated, I couldn't force the lock to release.

My snarl ripped through the room. So, they'd locked me up here instead of in the dungeon. Why?

A sharp smell hit my sinuses, and I growled, turning.

Maverna stood by the window dressed in a simple,

dark blue robe that hung to her feet. She eased back the hood, revealing her long gray hair.

"What do you want?" I asked, tired of this situation and tired of her. "Come to gloat?"

"Why would I gloat?"

"You made this happen. Did you kill the king?"

She shook her head, and her face tightened. "I didn't come here to talk about that."

"What if that's what I want to talk about?" There was more going on here than me being accused of murdering the king. Maverna was hiding something.

I first met her in a cave lining the cliffs on the edge of my estate. She'd told me to leave and, being friendly, I'd quizzed her about what she was doing. She'd laid a pattern in glossy stones on the dirt floor, and flames licked from one to the next.

She'd snarled and told me to forget what I'd seen, but stupid me, I'd stepped forward, accidentally scattering a second pattern of stones I'd missed.

Fury had filled her face, and her hands had lifted. She'd dropped the curse down on me like a boulder, then winked from view. I'd carried the burden of the curse since, and I still did not know why she'd done it.

"I came to tell you to stay away from the girl," she snarled.

"I won't do that. I love Raven, and I'm going to be with her no matter what anyone else says."

Her lips curled in an evil smile. "If you won't leave her, I might have to pay her a visit."

"Leave her alone," I snapped. Then I realized by

speaking, I gave myself away. "Why bother her?" I said casually, watching her out of the corner of my eye. "I'm locked in this room, and I cannot reach her." Was my charm strong enough to protect her? I didn't want to test it. What if . . . I couldn't think about that. I'd find a way to protect her. "I don't imagine I'll ever see Raven again."

Maverna's posture eased. "Then it has begun."

"What has begun?"

"Something far greater than you, Ice Lord."

Anger churned through me. She'd ruined my life. Ruined me. If she hadn't cursed me, I would be among the lords courting Raven. "I'm done with your games. I won't let you interfere with my life."

"You have no life other than the one I give you."

I stopped pacing and rubbed the wound on my leg she'd given to me at the same time as the curse. Healers throughout the kingdom applied magic, but the wound would seal over for only a short time before opening yet again. Why bother with something as simple as this?

I glared at her. "From what I can tell, you've ended my life already."

A chuckle shook her chest. "You don't enjoy my curse, do you? Right from the start, you've been in the way. This is the only way I can . . ." She bit down on her lips to hold back whatever else she might say.

"Either tell me everything or leave." I turned, though keeping her in view from the corner of my eye. What could she do to me other than kill me now or threaten Raven? I was rolling toward the edge of my life, and soon, I'd fall down the other side.

"I will not let you stand between me and what I've worked for." Her voice crackled, and her brow wrinkled with her frown. "You nearly ruined everything when you entered the cave. Ironic it was *you*."

"It was a mistake. I merely stepped forward."

"After I told you to leave. And despite the curse that should've taken you on a different path, you still pursue this one."

"Tell me what I did, and I'll make it right."

"It is too late. Once you are consumed by the curse, nothing will stop my plan."

Unless I broke it, something I was not going to mention. I'd found clues that suggested I could, but I wouldn't share that with her. I wasn't giving up yet.

"Did you come here to taunt me?" I asked. "If so, you can leave now."

"I find your current situation humorous." Her cackle rang out. "I didn't foresee *this*."

Telling her she wasn't much of a soothsayer wouldn't help my situation. I didn't need a second curse draped over the first.

Still, I couldn't help myself. I bent forward in a short bow, my words dripping with sarcasm. "I'm glad I could provide you with humor."

"Would you like to know more about the king?"

I tilted my head, studying her smooth face. Where was she going with this? "*You* murdered him, and it appears I'm about to pay for your crime."

"Aillun is conniving, isn't he?" she said with what I swore was pride.

"You sound proud of him. Why?"

"It all rests with him."

"Why are you proud of Aillun?" I demanded.

Mist began to take over her body, telling me she was leaving. Why had she come here? She'd barely taunted me and only about the curse. She'd told me to stay away from Raven, something I wouldn't do. And she was somehow connected to Aillun. Were they in this together?

The last was a random thought, but it stuck in mind.

I rushed toward her, determined to grab her and make her give me answers. But her form started to fade, and there was no holding onto smoke. My magical abilities may be strong, but they didn't extend to re-generating disappearing witches.

She laughed, savoring my irritation and confusion.

Before she completely winked out, she spoke one last time. "I'll give you one clue, though it's too late for it to be of any help. Ask Aillun where he put the king's body."

Reaching the area where she'd stood, I snarled and pawed at the air, but she'd left. In my mind, I tried to trace the path of her magic, but she'd sliced through the trail, leaving nothing to follow.

Turning, I strode back and forth at the end of my bed, analyzing everything she'd said, but I didn't come up with any answers.

The door opened, and one of the king's guards stepped into the room. A sweep of his hand bound my wrists and suppressed my magic. When one of the fae agreed to guard our liege lord, they were granted superior powers that came close to those bestowed on the king. Otherwise, anyone could get past the guards to our sovereign.

"The king will speak with you," the guard said.

A jolt went through me. "The king lives?"

"King *Aillun*."

Of course. He'd seized the throne. "I hadn't heard about the coronation."

The guard frowned. "You will come with me, or I will drag you to him."

"I have no reason not to walk with you." I flicked my fingers in his direction, though I couldn't add a spell to the gesture. "Shall we go?"

The guard watched me pace over to him, then led the way.

When we reached the ground floor, I thought of running, but I'd be pinned to the wall within seconds, and I had no interest in slamming my head again. I needed to know what was going on, and lying unconscious in my room would not give me answers.

The guard took me to the lavender room. After opening the door, he stepped to the side and dipped his head forward.

I strode inside, and he shut the panel behind me.

Like every other room named after a color, this one bloomed with a profusion of purple, from the small lounges strategically placed near the windows for someone to sit on, to the cushions and drapes.

Aillun—I could not call him my king—sat on a large,

ornate chair on the right side of the room, four guards flanking him on the dais.

All five of them watched as I strode near.

"There you are," Aillun said. "I wanted one last look at my father's murderer before you were put to death."

"Shouldn't I assume my guilt is not proven until my trial?" I asked blandly, though even I'd be foolish not to feel a surge of fear rising within me. This wasn't solely about my freedom. With me out of the way, Aillun could do whatever he wanted with Raven.

"I am the judge and jury," he said blandly. "I have convicted you."

This line of conversation would get me nowhere. "Why is Maverna interested in you?" I asked.

His right hand, sitting on the arm of the chair, twitched. With a curt nod, he sent the guard from the room, leaving us alone. He stood and stepped off the dais, striding past me.

"Maverna has no interest in me," he said. His words came out casually, but I detected a subtle shake in his voice.

"Is she related to you?" It was a wild guess on my part, but it struck true.

He froze, his back to me. "Why would you think that?"

So, not a denial? I scramble to find the right words to say. "No one knows who she truly is. Perhaps she's your sister?"

He spun, and a sarcastic smile rose on his face. "Do I appear her age? She is gray-haired. Old."

"You and I are the same age, and she is much older than *my* sister."

"Exactly. You know the king has no other children."

Despite his efforts to line up other heirs, the king had been unsuccessful, partly due to our slowing fae birthrate, but also due to sudden "accidents" among the three fae children born after Aillun.

I grinned, hoping it didn't come out shaky. Stunned, I was venturing into territory I'd never dreamed of before. "Then I can only assume Maverna must be your mother."

His teeth snapped together, but his smile widened. "My mother is dead, as you very well know. She lies in her tomb inside the family crypt."

"Does she? Or . . ."

"Or what?"

I took in his stiff posture and the way he almost seemed to stop breathing as he awaited my reply. Had my guess revealed something I'd never considered? If so, how horrifying. Everyone believed the queen died when he was born, but what if she'd left the kingdom instead?

Everything and everyone wore a mask here, even me with my scarred face I found difficult to hide.

I had no idea why.

"She abandoned you," I said, striking hard to drive home my guess.

"You don't know anything," he snarled, spittle flying, his arms flailing. "Anything!"

I set the thought aside for now, although I wasn't done tossing questions his way to see how he responded.

"Where is the king's body? Each king before him has been laid out for a viewing before burial."

"Your poison consumed his flesh. There will be no viewing."

And there was my answer. *Thank you, Maverna, for the suggestion.* She'd taunted me with a clue, believing I couldn't use it, but she was wrong.

Deep in my heart, I was convinced the king was *not* dead. I just needed to find him.

Chapter 35
Raven

Aillun tossed Elion against the wall. Elion's head hit with a crack, and he slid down the surface, collapsing on the floor.

Sobbing, I ran to him. I lifted him and cradled him in my arms, begging him to wake up.

He was breathing, but shit, he wasn't waking up!

"You bastard," I hurled at Aillun. Tears streaked down my face, and I hated them, because they implied weakness. I was anything but.

No, I could rampage as good as the next.

I carefully set Elion on the floor, rose, and slammed into Aillun.

No one had expected me to attack. After all, I was a weak human woman, right? Well, they hadn't had even a taste of my fury yet.

My hit sent him back against the wall. He released a horrified grunt. I smacked and kicked, determined to make him pay.

Within seconds, I was hauled away from him.

The head of the guard dragged me away from Aillun and frowned down at me. "How did you stop me?" He traced my face with his heavy gaze. "My magic should've kept you from touching him."

I wasn't revealing a damn thing.

"How dare you?" Aillun sputtered, swiping the blood off his face where my nails had dug a channel into his skin. My claws hadn't appeared, unfortunately, or I would've done a lot more damage. I would've ripped out his throat.

I shoved the guard away. "You're as bad as he is." I ran to Elion again, but someone hauled me away from him. They dragged me to my room and locked me inside.

Maecia showed up like this was a normal day, a tray of food in her hands that she set on a table near the window.

"What's happening?" I asked, my voice ragged from crying. "Where's Elion? Is he okay?"

She continued to say nothing, helping me dress in the day gown she'd brought earlier.

As she passed me, headed for the door, I grabbed her arm. "Tell me!"

Tears leaked down her cheeks, and she shook her head. She sliced across her lips with a finger.

"They cast a spell on you so you can't speak," I said dully. My shoulders drooped, and for one second, I wondered how I was going to fix this. My being here had endangered so many others.

Sniffing and wiping her eyes, she nodded.

"Is he alive?" I said with a whimper.

Her head bobbed up and down, and relief filled her eyes.

At least I could cling to that.

"Do you know where he is?" I asked.

She shook her head.

"I assume they locked him up somewhere. Can you find out where?"

Her head shook faster.

Damn.

"Can you get me out of this room?"

She moaned, her head jerking back and forth in a no.

"I'm sorry," I said. "I've made a mess, but I'm going to fix it."

Latching onto my shoulders, she gently shook me.

I pulled away. "Okay. I get it. Don't try to do anything. I . . . won't." There was no way I'd make this a promise. Let her think—and maybe tell the others—that I was going to behave and remain in my room, that they could strut me out in front of the other lords at the next soiree, and I'd pick one to marry.

Meanwhile, I'd be looking for opportunities to escape.

She left, and the door locked behind her.

While I had no appetite, I made myself sit in a chair and eat. My goal was to find Elion and leave this place, and I'd think better with a meal in my belly.

After finishing, I shoved the tray away and remained in a chair, staring out the window, contemplating ways to fix this. Where had they taken Elion? They'd stopped

Maecia from telling me, but if I could get out of here, I could search the place from top to bottom.

Was there a dungeon, and if so, how could I reach it? I assumed the king's guard would try to stop me, so I'd need a weapon, assuming weapons worked against fae magic.

I fingered the charm. Elion said it would block most magic, and it could provide a solid advantage. When he gave it to me, I bet he never thought I'd be using it in a mad rescue attempt to save him.

Voices echoed in the hall. I rushed to the panel, but the knob wouldn't turn.

I stomped back and forth inside my room for what felt like hours, periodically checking the windows that refused to open. Then an idea occurred to me.

After dressing in jeans, a t-shirt, and a hoodie, I went over to stand near the door and waited.

When Maecia returned for the tray and stepped inside the room, I wrenched the door open and fled out into the hall.

They must've trusted I'd behave, because they hadn't placed a guard.

I wasn't sure how to escape, but I was determined to take this opportunity.

Shouts rang out from my right, so I ran left. No one waited on the stairs, and I practically flew down them, though I slowed to a normal pace near the bottom to avoid detection.

Spying guards in the foyer, I waited until they weren't looking my way and slunk down the last flight of stairs. In seconds, I'd ducked around to the side, hugging the wall to avoid being seen.

I was about to make a mad dash toward the back hall on my left when a soft sound reached me.

Koko, the resha kit the king had given me, stood in the open doorway of a parlor opposite from where I stood. When he caught my eye, his tail puffed up over his spine, wagging. He made a soft whimper before turning and scooting into the room.

I peeked around the stairs, watching the guards. When they'd turned to pace in the opposite direction from me, I raced into the parlor and shut the door.

At least no one was using the room.

"Koko?" I whispered, peering around.

He leaped into my arms and snuggled my neck, releasing a rumbling purr.

"Oh, boy, little guy," I said softly, giving him tons of pats. I sunk down into a chair with a back facing the door and crouched low, tucking my legs up beneath me.

Koko struggled, so I released him, dropping him onto my lap. He rubbed against my hand and made soft cooing sounds.

"They've locked Elion up somewhere, and I don't know how to find him. And the king . . ." I didn't know why I was talking to a kit that wouldn't understand, but who else would listen to me now? "And now the king is dead."

After our last interaction, I hadn't thought very highly of the older fae, but still, tears sprang up in my eyes. He'd made demands of me and Elion, but they paled when compared to what Aillun might do next.

"What am I going to do?" I asked.

Koko made a soft chitter sound and hopped off my lap. He scampered across the room to the back left wall, then turned to look at me.

"I don't even know what I'm going to do with you. I'm kind of useless in all this."

Koko chittered again and pawed at an empty section of the wall.

"I mean, I don't have any magic. I'm—"

Koko cheeped loudly.

I frowned in his direction before getting up and striding over to the wall.

He tapped his paw on it.

"Is there a mouse in there?" Assuming he liked to hunt mice.

I swore he rolled his eyes. Rising up, he placed both front paws on the wall.

The smooth surface wavered, and I swore I saw an arched seam before Koko's paws dropped to the floor.

Only a normal wall was visible now.

Hold on.

"Is this some sort of magical secret door?" It was kind of convenient, but I wouldn't have entered this room if Koko hadn't found me.

I stooped down beside him and patted his head. "So, this might sound like I'm out of my mind, but is there a hidden door here?"

He rapped a paw on the wall again.

There was only one way to find out.

I placed both palms inside the area where I'd sworn I saw an arch and pushed.

The wall creaked and a door about the height of my knees and two feet wide glided inward, revealing a dark room.

Koko hopped through the opening, cooing.

I stared into the darkness for a second before crawling after him.

Chapter 36
Elion

Aillun snapped his fingers, and three guards stormed into the room. "Bind Elion and ensure he cannot get free."

I flung myself toward the window, but when I should've plunged through the glass, I hit it hard and fell to the floor. Standing, I shook my aching head and shuddered.

Aillun lifted one eyebrow my way. "Surely you realize I've had the room completely warded. Did you think I'd allow you to escape so easily?"

The guards cast spells that disabled my magic. Then they encircled my wrists with bindings and loosely linked my ankles. I could walk, but I would not be able to run.

When I tried to yank the restraints apart, shocks hit my skin. The scent of roasting flesh drifted up from my scorched skin. Magical bindings, then. There would be no breaking them, and if I guessed correctly, they were enhanced with spells to keep me from using my own magic against them.

I hated I couldn't fight back. Fear burst inside me, and a fine sweat broke out on my brow, but I kept my expression neutral, refusing to give anything away.

How would I get free? The tighter the noose, the harder it would be to slip from its grasp.

"Shall we take him to the dungeons?" a guard asked, latching onto my upper arm. "There is no better place than that for the one who killed the king."

"Leave him," Aillun said, watching my every move. His lips twitched, and I knew he hoped to see me squirm or explode in fury. "I'll place him where he'll never break free."

"He'll stand trial for murdering the king, correct?" the head of the guard, Garrik, asked. "The people deserve to see him die." He'd do whatever our new king asked, and while he was known as an honest fae who followed the rules, he would defer to whatever Aillun asked. He may not yet wear the crown, but Aillun was now our ruler.

"I watched him murder my father," Aillun said with horror and pain, jerking his head back and forth as if lost in the memory. "He poisoned him. Killed him. With such evidence, there is no need for Elion to stand trial. I have convicted him already."

Garrik stepped forward. "He deserves to die now!"

Aillun's hand lifted, and Garrik came to a shuddering halt. "You are correct. For his crime, he will suffer a torturous death."

My guts churned. I had to escape this trap.

Garrik bowed. "Pray we bring this about soon."

"Elion will be put to death for his actions," Aillun said blandly. "But let us wait three days to give our lords and ladies the chance to arrive for the event and bear witness. Everyone must know what happens to those who murder our sovereign king."

"Very well." Garrik bowed again. His gaze slid my way, and for the first time since I met this man years ago, hatred filled his eyes. "Do you have more need of us, my liege?"

"Tell the staff to prepare for my coronation. It will take place immediately after Elion faces the final punishment for his crime."

How did he plan to kill me? The norm was to be put on public display, then magically incinerated with a crowd in attendance to bear witness. It might be a quick death, but it would not be painless.

"Very well, my king," Garrik said, not looking my way.

Aillun grunted. "You may go."

The guards left, shutting the door behind them.

"Why not the dungeon?" I asked. There, I might stand a chance of escape.

"It's too easily accessible," Aillun said with a sly smile. "We wouldn't want you to get away, now would we? I have a much better place to secure you than the dungeons."

I sensed Maverna's involvement in all this. She'd

killed the king. If I was correct, she'd done so at Aillun's command.

A wave of his hand, and I was lifted off the floor. He left the dais and strode to a door at the back of the room and opened it.

I hovered above the ground as I was dragged behind him by magic.

He passed through three rooms, avoiding the hall outside the rooms, until we came to a little-used study three-quarters of the way down the left wing of the castle.

"Spells can be broken, as can bindings used by the guards," he said.

How did he know something like that? It was a tidbit I stored away. Perhaps there was a way out of this, after all.

I took in the room, finished with dark bronze wallpaper and drapes, plus nondescript furniture. A desk sat near the back right corner with a big chair waiting behind it. A big, round rug had been laid in the center of the floor. Why bring me here?

Aillun released a slick smile. He shifted furniture to the side with magic until he could expose the rug. When he rolled it up, he revealed a hatch on the floor.

He lifted it and dropped it onto the hardwood floor with a solid thud. A wooden ladder descended, though I couldn't see where it led.

"Inside," Aillun said. "In case you think you can get out of this; the room below is warded. I'm sure you'll be quite comfortable there while you wait."

He released the magic holding me suspended, and I

dropped to the floor, barely keeping my footing. I hobbled over to the hatch and looked down, taking in the small, bare chamber one level below.

"What, no bed, beverages, or food?" I asked. "You're not much of a host, Aillun."

He strode around behind me and shoved.

I fell feet-first into the hole and landed hard on the stone floor, collapsing onto my side.

The hatch banged closed above me.

Chapter 37
Raven

Crawling because I couldn't stand upright, I followed Koko down a steep slope that appeared to take us a few levels below the first floor of the castle. My eyes slowly adjusted to the darkness and while I couldn't see well, I could see the tunnel continued quite a distance ahead.

I continued crawling along the smooth stone floor, taking in the walls made of big slabs of rock curving up to the low ceiling. I rose to a crouch and hurried after Koko, who kept skipping ahead before turning back to wait for me to catch up.

"Where are you taking me, little guy?" I whispered. For all I knew, he came here regularly to hunt mice, and he wanted to share his next meal. Assuming there were mice in the fae kingdom. Was there such a thing as mice who can do magic?

Subtle scraping sounds ahead made my pulse pick up. Sweat broke out on my palms. I kept my steps light to avoid detection, breaking into an awkward, hunched forward jog to keep up with Koko.

The resha had a purpose, though I had no idea what it could be. But following this lead was better than sitting inside my room behind a locked door.

Who knew what I'd find down here?

A shudder tore through me at the thought of battling creatures out of a nightmare. I'd barely survived my battle with the cinder who killed the other human women.

Soft light bloomed ahead, but with some distance left to travel, I couldn't see much of anything. Did the passage exit the castle?

Koko kept going, waiting for me to catch up before sprinting ahead.

The tunnel ended, exiting into an intersection with a long stone wall opposite of where I hovered and passages extending to my left and right. I squinted before tiptoeing forward to study the arched door with a barred opening on the stone wall. I slowly rose to peek through the round metal grate at the top.

A cell? The room was about eight feet across, and the ceiling hung low, like the passage I'd just left.

Someone lay on a rusted metal bed sitting along the back wall. Unmoving, the person's back faced me. It wasn't Elion.

There was something familiar about the person's clothing, but I couldn't place where I'd seen it. Soil covered the fabric as if they'd been tossed onto the floor and dragged or they'd rolled in a freshly turned garden.

Koko sat by my feet, staring up at me sadly. Why had he brought me here? He perked up and chirped.

The person on the bed stirred and started to roll over to face me.

My pulse hammering in my throat, I ducked below the opening. My ragged breathing echoed around me.

"Hello?" the person said.

Damn. I'd recognize that voice almost anywhere.

"If someone is there, show yourself," they demanded in a haughty tone.

Yeah, he loved to command everyone around him.

I straightened and huffed. "Rumors of your death have been greatly exaggerated."

The king sat on the side of the bunk, smacking his boots on the dirt floor. "Get me out of here, Raven."

"How do you expect me to do that?" I grabbed the bars and yanked, but they remained solidly embedded in the stone.

I peered around but didn't see a knob. And there was no convenient key dangling from a hook on the wall. I had nothing to pry open the stone door.

"You're resilient. Stubborn," he said in a chipped voice. "Find a way." King Khaidill stood, though he had to remain hunched forward. When he began to topple forward, he slapped his palm against the wall and held himself steady.

"Everyone thinks you're dead, that Lord Elion poisoned you," I said. "They arrested him." Horror filled me all over again. I didn't know where he was or if he was okay. I needed to find him.

But I couldn't leave the king here. He was alive, which proved Elion didn't murder him.

"Someone poisoned me," King Khaidill said. "But it was not Elion."

"The only other people in the room were the witch, who popped in only long enough to make threats before disappearing, and your son."

"Ah, yes, my beloved son," he said with a snarl.

"You don't sound happy with him at the moment."

"I do not plan to discuss this with you."

I propped my fist on my hip. "Because I'm a lowly human?"

He huffed out a sigh. "Because we're wasting time. I need to get out of here immediately, or I truly *will* be dead."

My irritation dropped away. "I bet Aillun did it. He's pronounced himself king and took Elion somewhere. I've been trying to find him."

"It would not surprise me to hear Aillun was involved." He sat back on the bunk and rubbed his face before raking his fingers through his black hair shot through with silver. When he looked up at me, sorrow filled his deep blue eyes. "Aillun has been encouraging me to step down from the throne to allow him to rule instead. As my only heir, he would like to take command while he's still young, he said."

"Rather than wait for you to die of old age, he poisoned you."

"*Tried* to poison me. I warded myself long ago with spells to prevent poison from taking full effect. I believe your assumption is correct, however. Aillun put something in my drink. Instead of killing me, it knocked me unconscious. The healers, however, brought me here, which I would not have expected."

"They're in on the plan."

"That is my belief."

"Your elite guards as well?" How deep did this go?

"I fear this is also true," he said sadly. "Everyone appears eager to see Aillun take my place on the throne."

"A son who tried to murder you."

"Ah, yes, that's the interesting thing about all this." A frown filled his face. "I do not believe . . ."

I lifted Koko into my arms and waited for the king to continue.

He studied my face for a long time, as if trying to decide if he dared speak further. Finally, he cleared his throat and stiffened his spine.

"I've suspected for some time that Aillun is not my true son."

Chapter 38
Elion

I landed hard on the stone floor, remaining still for a moment to make sure I hadn't broken something. But nothing felt injured.

I scrambled to my feet and climbed the ladder, but no matter how hard I slammed my shoulder against the hatch, it didn't open. Aillun must've magically locked it.

A careful study of the walls with my hands showed there was no way out of this hole. I hadn't heard there were hidden locations like this within the castle, but Aillun grew up here. As a child, he must've explored and found it.

With a growl, I sat with my back against the wall, my knees bent. I stared around, hoping to find a way out I'd missed.

I dozed . . .

"Ah, now this is so much fun," someone said, waking me.

I sat up and rubbed my head with my bound hands.

"What do you want, Maverna?" I couldn't see her, but there was no mistaking her crotchety voice.

"I only stopped in for one thing."

A long silence followed, but I waited her out. She wanted me to beg, to ask her what that one thing was, but I refused to give her the satisfaction.

Finally, she grunted. "I've decided to change your curse."

"Remove it. I promise I'll leave you alone."

"You do not know where I'm hiding. Of course you'll leave me alone."

I loved that she sounded affronted. I'd do anything to drive a negative emotion from her. It was the least I could do after she ruined my life.

"Don't you want to know what I'm planning to do?"

I didn't sense a change. "You're toying with me."

"Oh, never that."

"Why did you abandon your son?" I asked, holding my breath while I awaited her answer.

"You know nothing," she barked.

"Because you tell me nothing. Let me share with you what I've guessed."

Now she was the one holding her breath. I sensed more than heard it, and the idea I could control even this little thing sent a thrill through me.

"Speak," she snarled. "Or I will leave."

"Without altering my curse?" In the dark, I didn't need to hide my conniving grin.

"Speak!"

Oh, to finally have the chance to play games with her.

Sadly, I was trapped here, and nothing was going to come from this game.

"You're Aillun's mother. You abandoned him, and now you've returned to help him seize the throne."

She said nothing for a very long time. "Why would you think this?" In her voice, I heard confirmation of my guess. The change in her tone was subtle, but it was enough.

"Aillun told me," I said.

"You lie," she hissed.

"Perhaps I do, and perhaps I don't. Since he intends to murder me within days, it hardly matters, does it?"

"He shouldn't do that. You need to die from the curse."

"I have plenty of time left for that," I said blandly. "I'll be long dead before then. Who would've thought?" Wait . . . "Why do I need to die from the curse?"

"It's the only way to kill you."

"It appears I might be very easy to kill."

"Your mother cast a spell on you that protects you. Only—" She paused as if listening, but I heard nothing except my breathing and the subtle shift of her feet on the floor.

Her magic hit me, jolting through me.

"What have you done?" I snarled.

"You will now die in fourteen days." She said it so simply, as if my death was no different than sweeping up refuse from the floor and tossing it away.

What did she mean about my mother protecting me? My mother had never come across as a very loving person, and definitely not one who'd cast spells to keep her children safe.

"Altering the curse is all I can do to prevent . . ."

"Always a few clues but never the complete answer." I was done with her. I needed to scan my body and figure out what she'd done. "You should go. I'd like to catch up on my rest." Frustration boiled inside me. I needed to know what was going on, not be teased, but Maverna would never share everything.

Pausing, I listened. She'd gone.

I growled, but giving into my irritation would not bring her back or give me answers.

Fourteen days? What did she mean by that?

Then I realized what she'd meant.

Even if I could escape Aillun's plan, instead of dying in one year, I now only had fourteen days left to live.

Despair roared through me, and I slumped against the wall.

"Lord Elion," someone whispered sometime later.

"Go away, Maverna. Although, I might welcome a bit more teasing. Each piece of the puzzle gives me a better view of the picture."

"Lord Elion?" the person cried out.

It wasn't Maverna.

"Follen," I shouted, getting to my feet. I clambered up the ladder and banged my fists on the hatch, cursing the magical bands that kept my wrists and ankles bound.

I kept slamming my hands against the wooden surface until the hatch lifted.

"Ah, there you are, sir," Follen said in a cheery voice.

"I've drawn your bath. Would you like a meal sent to your room as well?"

I welcomed the twinkle in his eye and his sharp humor. "I believe I will forego the meal for now. I do hope that is all right."

Follen bowed. "Of course, sir."

He helped me climb out of the stone room, then closed the hatch and laid the rug back in place. "When you disappeared from your room and no one could tell me where you'd gone, I had to find you."

He leaned near and dropped his voice. "There are so many odd things happening inside the castle. I could never believe . . ." He shook his head. "I am not completely sure what to think, but I know one thing. You did not kill the king."

Sighing with relief, I gripped his shoulder. "Thank you, friend."

"However, I believe it would be unwise for you to remain within the kingdom for long," he said. "Perhaps there is a place you can escape to where you can decide what can be done next to help the kingdom?"

"I will return to my estates, but I'm not going anywhere without Raven." Fourteen days. The words sliced through me. It wasn't enough time.

"I understand." His gaze traveled to the bindings on my wrists and ankles. His eyes closed tightly, and he murmured something in elvish, a language only his people understood. Unless a fae had at least half elf blood, they were not allowed to learn it.

A soft chuckle behind me sent me spinning.

"Well, well, well. It looks as if you are in a *bind*, Ice Lord," Erleene said with a kind smile.

After shooting a look of thanks to Follen, I held up my hands toward the elf witch. "Can you break them?"

She huffed, insulted I might doubt her ability to diffuse Aillun's magic. A nod, and the magical bindings disappeared.

"Thank you." I rubbed my wrists. "You're right, Follen. I cannot stay within the kingdom. Aillun has seized the throne and accused me of the king's murder."

"He is making plans for his coronation and your punishment already," Follen said with a shudder. He peered around, but we remained alone in the parlor. "I do not believe it is wise for you to stay in this location for long."

"Can you take me to Raven?" I asked. I wouldn't leave without her.

"That will be a problem," Follen said. "She has disappeared."

Erleene chuckled. "She had not disappeared; she is with her resha kit."

"Everyone is in an uproar after what happened with the other human females, and they are determined to locate Raven and take her to the new king," Follen said. "The two women who wished to leave are gone, and Aillun has put a halt to anyone else traveling here from the human realm."

I wasn't surprised. Aillun had opposed the bride plan from the beginning.

"I'll find Raven before anyone else." The thought of

her in danger terrified me. I started across the room, heading for the hall.

"Do not try to stop her," Erleene warned. "What she does now could very well save the kingdom."

Fear coursed through me, and I turned back to face the witch. "Is she in danger?" Keeping her safe was my primary goal. Only once I'd placed her in a secure location could I return here to confront Aillun.

"Aren't we all in danger?" she asked wryly.

"Do you know who she is?" I asked softly. "*What* she is?" She'd slashed Nuvian with claws that disappeared immediately after she'd used them. She'd been afraid of what this might mean. I didn't care who she was; I only wanted to be with her. But if knowledge of her past could help us, I needed to hear it.

"That will be revealed in due time," Erleene said.

Demanding the witch give me an answer would get me nowhere. I didn't have time to play cryptic games. "Why don't you save the kingdom instead of leaving it to others?" I asked with a wry twist of my lips.

Her magic was so much greater than mine. With a flick of her finger, she could make this right.

"You know we are not allowed to interfere," Follen said. Not the curse, however. She'd tried and was unable to break it.

"Yet you just freed me," I said.

"This is but a small favor," Erleene said. "It will not influence what comes next." She chuckled again. "Would you rather Follen left you to rot in the hole?" She smoothed her long gray hair off her shoulder, leaving it to hang down her back. She had dressed in another robe, this one in dark blue. It hung to her toes. "We do what we can and what we must."

"Aillun must not take the throne," I said. "Our world will be in great danger if he does."

"What must come to pass cannot be halted," she said. "And you, my Ice Lord, have your own path to follow. Leave Aillun to those who will best see him pay for what he has done already and will still do." She nodded to Follen. "Take the Ice Lord to the woods and wait there. I will ensure Raven joins you. They must be together, or all may be lost."

I wanted to quiz her about her mysterious statements, but she owed me nothing. And she was correct; the elves would watch what happened here, but they wouldn't interfere unless it was going to affect them.

Erleene disappeared, and Follen tilted his head to the door on the back side of the parlor. We could pass through the rooms to the back of the castle and escape to the woods.

As we kept close to the gardens, hurrying across the back lawn, I could only hope Raven was safe and that she'd join me soon.

I didn't care what Erleene said about interference.

If Raven didn't arrive within a short time, I would storm the castle to find her.

Chapter 39
Raven

"What makes you believe Aillun isn't your son?" I asked the king.

He sighed and scrubbed his face with his palms. "I'm not really sure. It's just a feeling I've had since Aillun was young."

"You raised him. That makes him your son, no matter what."

"You are correct. This is not solely about blood, of course. I've loved Aillun from the moment he drew in his first breath."

"Were you there when he was born?"

He looked up. "I was not. My wife, my beloved queen, was away when she went into labor. She died giving birth to Aillun. Her ladies brought Aillun and my wife's body to the castle when it was safe to travel. We buried my wife, and I raised my son."

"Why do you suspect he's not yours?"

He lifted his chin. "I cannot name the reason. It is something I feel within my heart."

"I can understand why you'd want to disown him. He's a nasty, conniving, slimy guy."

His chuckle rang out. "This is why I gave you the resha kit. You have spirit." He nudged his chin to Koko purring in my arms. "Ask him to help free me."

I wasn't sure how my pet could open a cell, but he'd understood my need to find the king. Reshas were special.

"Why haven't you been able to escape on your own?" I asked. "Wave your hand and unlock the door. I'll show you the way to the first floor. We'll confront Aillun in front of everyone, and you'll be restored to your rightful place on the throne. You can do what you want with Aillun from there, though I suggest you do something that keeps him from trying to steal the crown from you a second time."

"Perhaps that is why I believe he is not my true son. I do not like the idea that he could come from my loins, that I could give him everything in my heart, and he still grew into a greedy, conniving person."

I shrugged. "It happens. Nature versus nurture. You can only do so much with the gene pool you're given. Power also corrupts. I'm sure you did what you could, but everyone around Aillun must cater to his whims. He saw that early and took advantage of it."

"I should've sent him far from the castle, fostered him with someone who would keep him from this corruption you name. But I was weak. He was the only part of my beloved mate I had left, and I couldn't bear to send him away."

"Well, here we are. You're behind magical bars. He's solidifying his power upstairs. Show me how to free you, and we'll end his short reign. Use the boost of magic I heard you were given when you were crowned."

"My boost of power, as you call it, is gone."

"What happened to it?"

"Aillun cast a spell that suppresses it."

I set Koko down and started pacing in front of the cell. There had to be a solution here. Good always triumphed over evil, right? Or evil won and rewrote history—that was a common occurrence where I came from. The fae kingdom was probably no different. But I wasn't going to be a glass half full person today. Nope, my cup still held a lot of promise.

What to do . . . My mysterious claws that appeared at convenient times, then disappeared, would be useless here. I also had a charm from Elion that muted magic directed my way.

Wait . . . My charm.

He'd told me not to remove it, but . . .

I lifted the chain over my head and held it through the bars. "Put this on."

"A necklace?"

Frustration made me snappy. "Just do it. I want to try something. I'm going to keep my fingers on the stone, however. Elion told me never to remove it, but I'll stretch that rule a bit here."

He sighed but rose, and hunched over, dropped the chain over his head.

The king's frown faded. "Oh, my."

I grinned. "I assume you're okay with trying on my necklace now."

"My power has returned."

"As long as you're wearing my necklace, Aillun's spell is suppressed. Maybe now you can get yourself out of here."

With a grunt, he lifted his hands. The door shimmered before completely disappearing. One of these days, I wanted to ask everyone where things went when they were no longer in view.

The king strode into the hall, and I trotted beside him, maintaining contact with the charm.

"Take me to the throne room. I have a usurper to confront," he said with his usual slightly conceited spunk. Guys in power never changed. However, he'd come across as a decent guy, other than during what I hoped was a momentary aberration on his part related to me and Elion.

The king owed me, and I knew just how he could pay me back.

"Please tell me you're going to do more than just confront Aillun." I wanted to see the king magically smack his supposed son around. "And don't forget Elion. We need to make sure he's released."

The king paused in the hall, his lips twisting. "You truly love that cursed beast?"

I snarled. "Don't be nasty. I just rescued you." I held out my other hand. "Chain, please. I want it back."

He lifted it off and dropped it over my head. I felt better once the stone had settled between my breasts.

Koko skipped around at our feet, and I swore he looked anxious. Stooping forward, I lifted him, holding him close. His tiny heart pattered, and he whimpered.

"It's okay, little guy," I said. He must be stressed by all this activity. He usually spent his days playing with his littermates, not rescuing kings from secret dungeons.

"Lead me out of here," the king said, his spine stiff, an awkward position considering he couldn't fully stand up straight. "As for you and Lord Elion . . ." He huffed out a sigh. "I suppose I could relent and allow him to remain in the castle."

"How generous of you."

He missed my sarcasm. "As for you two being together . . . I will need time to think on it."

"We're going to do what we want."

His spine stiffened. "I am king."

"Not at the moment."

"All right, then," he growled. "Help me, and I will permit you two to . . . You do realize he's cursed."

"I'm going to break it."

"That is impossible," he said sadly. "He is not the only one who has consulted everyone for a way to remove it."

"I'll find a way." My words came out strong, but I shook inside. I'd try, but what if trying wasn't enough?

This wasn't a fairytale where good would always triumph in the end. I could love him desperately and still lose him.

He stared at me in awe. "You do love him."

"I just said that didn't I?"

"Then I grant my permission for you to be together."

"Thanks." A hurdle out of the way, though I might never see Elion again, and it gutted me. But I wasn't going to think about that now. I waved to the passage I'd traveled from. "I came from that direction. You may need to crawl."

He scowled, probably put out at the thought of getting his hands and knees dirty. But why be picky now? Crawling beat sitting in a locked cell.

I led the way, with Koko scooting ahead of me, looking back at us with grave concern. Something was wrong, but I couldn't figure out what the problem could be.

Unease zipped up my spine, but I was on the right track, so I shut it down.

Everything would be resolved soon. The king would take back his throne, punish—or, hey, why not banish?—Aillun. He'd free Elion, and we could finally be together. Once things had completely settled, I could send for my sister. Would she enjoy growing up surrounded by fae magic?

We stumbled out into the parlor on the first level of the castle.

With Koko in my arms, who was now strangely calm, I followed the king into the hall. He strode quickly to his main throne room, probably believing he'd find Aillun there.

We came across Axilya in the hall outside the throne room.

Her gaze skimmed across the king, and she dismissed him with a huff, focusing on me. "There you are. I've been looking everywhere for you. The king wants to speak with you immediately."

I blinked at her, surprised she didn't bow to King Khaidill, let alone call Aillun king when the real guy stood nearby.

"Why don't you take us to Aillun, then," I said, picking something neutral to focus on. That unease I'd shrugged aside returned with a shocking jolt.

Something weird was going on here.

"Very well," Axilya said, latching onto my arm. She marched me toward the throne room.

The king frowned at Axilya before following us.

He kept flicking his fingers at her, and his frown deepened. Was he casting—or trying to cast—spells on her? If so, I got the feeling they weren't working.

Axilya swept open the door to the throne room and strode inside. "I have located the human female, your highness." She dipped forward in a deep bow. "I found her in the hall with this male I haven't seen before in my life."

Aillun sat on the throne at the end of the enormous, gilded room. Fae lords crowded along both sides of the room, staring at me.

As Axilya dragged me toward the throne, Aillun

stood. His gaze skimmed over me and landed on King Khaidill. While Axilya might not recognize the king, it was clear Aillun did by the way his jaw dropped.

What was going on here?

Oh . . . I tugged my charm over my head and placed it on the floor just out of touch, then turned to the king.

A male I'd never seen before stood a few feet away. This couldn't be possible unless Aillun had cast a devious spell on his father or the entire kingdom.

From the puzzled looks directed our way, no one else recognized the true king. His eyes widened as the same realization sunk in.

"They don't see me as me," he whispered.

I grabbed my chain, but when I rushed toward the king to put it over his head and suspend the spell, Aillun leaped off the dais and grabbed my arm, holding me back.

"Stop them," he cried, while I struggled to break free. "Capture that fae male. He tried to kidnap this woman."

If I could get the king out of here, I could loan him my necklace. Then he could show them who he truly was. But Aillun would do anything to stop me.

I wrenched away from his grasp and ran, darting around lords trying to stop me. Grabbing the king's arm, I dragged him toward the door with pandemonium erupting around us.

We bolted into the hall.

And slammed into a wall of guards.

Chapter 40
Elion

"Where is Erleene?" I asked, pacing back and forth. Limping, that is. As always, the damn wound I received when she bestowed her curse ached. It hadn't healed, and I suspected it would still bother me on the day the curse sucked me into its deadly embrace. My only hope was it would heal if I could break the curse.

"She will be here," Follen said, watching the path. "Never fear. When she arrives, she will have Raven with her. She would never leave our..."

"Your what?"

"It is nothing."

"You started to say something."

"And I cannot finish the thought. Please accept this."

I grumbled, but I couldn't force him to speak if he didn't want to. Or if he *couldn't* share.

We waited in a tiny meadow on the other side of a large clump of thorny bushes. While we could see the path through the sparsely leafed branches, I doubted anyone passing would see us unless they directly looked our way.

The air shimmered beside us, and Erleene appeared —without Raven.

I stormed up to her, ignoring my sore leg. "Where is she?"

"Can you be patient?" she asked with a roll of her eyes. "I dipped into the castle, though I kept myself hidden, but I couldn't collect her. She was a tad busy with the king's guards."

They'd caught her. I knew it. Leaving them, I stomped around the thicket to reach the path.

Erleene appeared in front of me, blocking my way.

Few of the fae could move through the inner realm, a dark place full of corridors and screams. It was unwise to travel there long, or you could be stuck in the realm's sinister clutches forever.

However, the inner realm gave those with the right magic a way to travel to distant locations in a blink of time. I'd experimented with it but hadn't perfected the magic well enough to use it more than in practice. If I popped into view in front of someone I shouldn't, I'd be captured all over again.

Next time, Aillun would not allow me to escape.

Follen joined us, humor shining in his eyes.

"Raven will join us soon enough," Erleene said. "I would not leave her in true danger."

"If the guards have her, she won't be able to escape." I struggled to hold on to my temper. I wanted to gnash my teeth and blast my way into the castle to find her.

She smiled. "You think she is not capable of escaping a few guards?"

"You speak of her claws. Of what she could be."

Her head dipped forward. "She is also resourceful. It was bred into her. Never doubt that."

"Take me to her?" I'd beg if it meant I could help Raven.

"Now there is an interesting idea." She cocked her head as if listening—or looking ahead. I'd heard she could foretell the future on occasion. Many tried but did so without any accuracy.

She held up her finger when I started to speak, before nodding. "I will take you to a location not far from her. From there, you should all be able to escape the castle."

"I will wait here," Follen said, his gaze locked on Erleene. "I have no wish to travel through the inner realm right now, although she is—"

"Yes, you shouldn't go with us," Erleene held out her hand to me. "Come along. We don't have much time."

I bit back a growl. If there wasn't time, why had she told me to wait here patiently? It wouldn't do me any good to ask.

She closed her eyes. "I suggest you also block out what you might see within the realm."

This was why I didn't dare test my own skills with this form of travel. It was difficult to locate a destination if you couldn't see where you were going. Only the most skilled could do this with their eyes open.

With my eyes closed, I could be standing anywhere. But the air changed, and I smelled smoke. I opened my eyes to find us floating through a world unlike anything I'd seen before.

A shriek rang out to our right, and Erleene's hand tightened on mine.

We dropped onto a stone floor hard, and as I placed my hand on the wall to keep my balance, I recognized one of the long hallways inside the castle.

The door at the opposite end banged open. Raven and a male fae I'd never seen before burst through, racing this way.

"Elion," Raven cried with relief. Her resha kit, Koko, scampered at her heels, shooting terrified looks over his shoulder.

I ran to her, lifted her, and kissed her.

She laughed around my kiss. Holding my face, she tugged her face away. "Later, dude. We need to get out of here."

Guards entered the hallway. Spying me, their cries erupted.

I thought of shifting in to my wolf form, but there wasn't time.

"Capture them," Aillun bellowed from the hall. "Do not let them get away. Kill them if you must."

I lowered Raven to the floor but held her hand tightly in mine. We wouldn't be separated again.

"We must leave now," Erleene shouted, her wide eyes taking in the king's guard and Aillun rushing down the hall.

With Raven close, I ran toward Erleene, but I faltered when I spied the king following us. He lived! I knew he was still alive. How had he met up with Raven?

"Keep going, boy," he bellowed, waving for Koko to race ahead of us. The creature kept snarling at the guards. "Don't let them catch us."

This wasn't possible, but the stranger was gone. Where had the king come from?

"A spell," Raven said, catching the confusion on my face. She held up our linked hands.

The charm deactivated the spell, revealing the stranger was the king.

Raven's wild gaze spun to the guards behind us. "We've gotta go."

We flung ourselves through a back door and stumbled out onto the lawn.

"Run into the woods," Erleene said from inside the castle. "I cannot go with you further, but I will slow the guards."

I didn't pause to ask questions but raced across the back lawn toward the path. The sound of her magic meeting the guards rang out until a sudden silence descended.

I wanted to turn back to help her, but I needed to get Raven and the king to safety.

Magic hit the ground around us, telling me the king's guard would capture us within seconds. They quickly adjusted their aim, but due to Raven's charm, most of the attack deflected off us. The king staggered and groaned, pressing his palm against the back of his thigh.

Koko snarled at the guards, but he was tiny; there wasn't anything even a protective resha kit could do.

"Go," he cried. "I will fix this."

There wasn't time for anything like that. Aillun must've done something to suppress his powerful magic. At this point, would the guard stop if they saw the true king? They could've been swayed already by Aillun.

Raven took the king's hand and dragged him along with us. He hobbled but kept up. With a connection to Erleene's charm, the magic hit us like the stings of bees, but it didn't slow our pace.

When we reached the woods, we raced down the path, calling softly to Follen as we came to the thorn thicket. He frowned at the king but didn't ask questions.

"Raven," Follen said, giving her a quick bow. He and Erleene shared a heavy glance I couldn't interpret, but there was no time for questions.

Follen waved for us to continue running, his hands lifting and his eyes sliding closed.

I looked back as we started along a curve in the path. Follen mumbled in elfish, and a shimmering wall appeared between us and the guard. As they slammed into it, he melted back into the woods, disappearing from view, only to burst out of the brush ahead of us on the path.

"Quickly," he said, nudging his head to a dark opening in the dense brush on his right. We snaked down a narrow trail that curved back and forth before arriving at the base of a cliff. He led us up a tight switchback trail that ended at a cave. I didn't remember seeing one here, but I trusted Follen with my life.

Raven scooped up Koko and held him close as we rushed through the arched opening.

Chapter 41
Raven

We walked through a dark cave, our footsteps nearly silent on the dirt-covered floor. At the back, we entered a long tunnel with a stone ceiling two stories above. The walls tightened around us.

Follen snapped his finger, and small lights appeared, hovering things that floated at waist level to guide our way.

Koko licked my chin, and I snuggled him close, giving him lots of pets while he purred. I was grateful he'd not only helped me rescue the king, but that he'd remained with me. He wiggled, and I put him down, smiling as he scampered ahead to catch up with the king.

A steady drip rang out far ahead, and a damp feeling hung in the air.

I didn't dare say a word. The guards had been so close behind us I'd felt their furious breathing on my neck. Would they find the cave and follow?

The king and Follen walked ahead of us. They spoke

in low voices, and I couldn't make out what they were saying.

"Koko led me to the king," I said. "I helped him escape and . . ." I shot him a wild smile. "He gave his permission for us to be together."

"I didn't need permission."

"Not truly, but it helps if he's not against us, don't you think?"

"You're right. It does." He tugged me close with an arm around my shoulders and kissed the top of my head.

"I missed you," he whispered. "I was terrified something would happen to you."

Pausing, I buried my face in his chest, drinking in his scent of fresh air and promises. "I was afraid I'd never see you again."

His arms enfolded me, holding me close. "I'll find you no matter where you are, Raven. Trust this."

The pain in my heart eased, though nothing would take away the fear I'd felt when I thought I'd lost him forever.

"Kiss me quick." I nudged my head toward the king and Follen. "Then we need to catch up to them."

He lifted me off my feet, and his mouth met mine, plundering, showing me how much he wanted and needed me.

I stroked his neck, wishing we were alone, and we wore nothing. I'd had a taste of him, and I wanted more.

His tongue stroked mine, igniting each of my cells, one after another. A moan burst from me, and he lifted his head.

"Raven." He spoke with so much emotion that tears sprang up in my eyes. Happy tears, not sad. I had no reason to mourn.

"We need to go," Follen said, coming back to stand beside us with concern creasing his face. The king remained farther down the tunnel with Koko, and I sensed the king's impatience.

When I slid down Elion's body, he gave me a heady smile. Soon, we'd be alone, and I'd show him how much I'd missed him.

He took my hand, and we followed the others. The tunnel sloped upward, and I wondered where we were going.

"Why aren't the guards following?" I whispered. "I'm glad they're not, but wouldn't they have seen us entering the cave?"

"Erleene slowed them, and Follen hid the opening. I imagine they're still trying to find our trail." He explained how Follen had freed him from a hidden room beneath a little-used parlor and how Aillun had planned to murder him in front of all the lords.

I couldn't stop trembling at the thought of how close I'd come to losing him. How I could still lose him. We weren't free yet, and with magic, anyone could pop into the tunnel and take us back to the castle. Elion would be put to death, and I'd be forced to marry one of the other lords.

"They can't follow us here using magic, can they?" I asked, peering around in true fear. Without magic, I was essentially useless. Elion would do anything to protect me; he'd die to keep me safe. And that scared me almost as much as the thought of Aillun appearing in front of us and binding us with magic.

"Follen has cast a confusion spell to make it hard for them to track us."

Maybe we *would* get away. That thought perked me up a bit more.

Elion picked up his pace until we walked close enough behind Follen and the king that I could touch them if I chose.

He didn't say anything for a long time, and I swore he kept shooting me sad looks.

"We're going to your estate, right?" I asked.

"Yes, we are." Tension thrived in his voice.

Others called it the Ice Castle, and I'd wondered why. I'd soon find out, but it didn't matter if he lived in a shack. I wanted to be with him no matter where he went.

I squeezed his hand. "It'll be okay."

His head jerked in a nod, but for some reason, he dragged his gaze away from mine again.

"What's wrong?"

He shook his head and stared forward.

Worry took root in my gut, and it churned with dismay. Something was happening, but he didn't want to tell me.

I had no choice but to let it go. Maybe he was tired from being trapped in a small room. He'd been accused of murder. The last thing he could think of at a time like that was us.

No matter what, he still wanted me. This was embedded in my soul.

We walked for hours, finally leaving the cave at the top of a mountain that was one of many in a long-range stretching in both directions. A cliff dove sharply in front of us, and a tiny trail zigzagged from here toward the bottom.

"Down," Follen said.

The king remained where he was. "I will leave you here. I must travel my own path now."

"Where will you go?" Elion asked.

"It is time I paid Maverna a visit."

"No . . ." Follen blanched and grabbed the king's arm. "It is too dangerous."

The king stared at Follen's hand until he released the king. "You would tell me what I must and must not do?"

"We need you," Elion said in a reasonable tone. "The entire kingdom needs you. Why challenge Maverna now?"

"You know why," he said to me.

He wanted to ask her if Aillun was his true son. Did Elion know what the king suspected? I doubted it.

I wanted to release the words, set them free on the world, but it wasn't my secret to tell. If the king chose to hold this information back, he had a good reason.

"She tried to poison you," Elion said. "She will succeed if you give her a second chance."

"You cannot stop me," the king said.

"But I must." Follen's hands lifted and magic

crackled across the tips of his fingers. In seconds, the king lay on the ground, unconscious.

"What did you do to him?" Elion cried, rushing toward Follen.

Follen held out his palm, and Elion ran into an invisible wall. "I did what I must. He cannot go to Maverna. Too much is at play in what happens next. Besides, Aillun has stolen the power that comes with the throne. Without that power, he will be no match for Maverna."

Elion's eyes widened. "How was Aillun able to do that?"

Follen shook his head. "He had help. He will do anything to solidify his reign."

"Maverna is helping Aillun," I said, and the two males nodded.

"It's still not right to cast a spell to make him unconscious," Elion said. "He's the king. He makes his own decisions."

"He's not infallible. He makes mistakes," Follen said. He lifted the king with magic, and turning, started down the trail with the king floating behind him. "Come. We have a long way to travel before nightfall."

Koko snarled as he his gaze flicked between the king and Follen. I picked him up and held him while his little body shook. He was frightened, but I also sensed he was angry. At Follen or the king?

Elion shot me a look of dismay. I could tell he ached to help the king, but from what I'd learned, he trusted Follen implicitly. His lips tightened, but the worry didn't leave his face.

"All right," he said softly for my ears alone. "I'll permit this for now."

By the time we reached the bottom of the cliff, the sun had been engulfed by the horizon, leaving only blades of pink and yellow stabbing up into the sky. Follen led us to an enormous tree with broad, needled branches sweeping low enough to touch the ground in a circle around it. He lifted a branch and waved for us to step beneath, floating the king beside us.

He'd set up a small camp at the base of the enormous trunk, complete with three small tents, a firepit, and a wooden crate that must hold supplies.

"We will stay here tonight," Follen said, using magic to open the flap on one of the tents and placing the king on a cot inside.

Whimpering, Koko leaped from my arms and scampered into the tent.

"Wake him," Elion said. "You have used magic long enough. He must be allowed to have a say in his own destiny."

"I will do so in the morning, and when I'm confident he won't do something foolish."

"I feel as if I don't know you." Shock bled through Elion's words.

I took his hand and held it.

"I am who I have always been," Follen said. "But I am also Erleene's brother."

Elion's eyes widened. "You . . . No. It cannot be true."

"I do not have her abilities of sight, but she shares what she sees with me. The king must not go to Maverna until the right time." He gripped Elion's arm. "Please, friend. Trust me in this. There is so much more involved here than you know."

"Tell me everything."

Sorrow filled Follen's face, and he shot a look my way I couldn't interpret. "I cannot. Please believe I share what I can."

Elion growled, his hands forming fists at his sides. "I don't like this, but I trust Erleene."

He didn't name Follen, and I didn't blame him. Follen had kept this vital information hidden. Elion must feel horribly betrayed.

Follen didn't wait for Elion to speak further. He bustled around the campsite, using magic to light a fire and prepare a quick meal with ingredients from the chest.

We went to bed after that. I joined Elion in one of the tents, determined not to be parted from him again.

I wanted to love him fully, to show him how much he meant to me. My need was a raging beast inside me, and it ached to be set free. But the last thing I wanted was for Follen to hear.

He held me and kissed me tenderly. "I love you, Raven," he whispered as I started to drift off. "Remember that, no matter what."

I wanted to ask him what he meant, but my eyes . . .

I woke at dawn to Follen's cry outside our tent. We rushed out to find him standing near the cold firepit. Koko sat on the ground beside him, whimpering.

"The king is gone," he said.

Elion shifted into his wolf form and sniffed the area. When he became his fae self again, dismay filled his eyes. He pointed into the densest part of the woods. "He took this path on foot."

"I must go after him before it is too late. Without his full power . . ." His gaze shot to me. "Take Raven to your Ice Castle. I sense the answers you both seek will be found there."

A blink, and Follen disappeared.

Chapter 42
Elion

We entered my property. Soon, we'd see the castle where I'd lived after I was cursed. My new life had begun in the cave at the back of the estate.

"It's . . ." Raven turned wide eyes my way. "I don't understand." She stepped back over the invisible line marking the edge of my estate and the one next door, her shoes sinking into lush grass. Plants grew in perfusion there but not here.

"It' been like this since I was cursed." I'd shared what happened in the cave, but neither of us could determine why Maverna had been so angry. I'd interrupted a spell, but why doom me to live in a world of ice until my untimely death?

Maybe torture is the point, Raven had said.

When she stepped back onto my property, her shoes crunched on frozen ground. Icicles hung from stark, leafless branches in the forest and snow fell softly around us.

A gust of wind swept a bit of snow across the border between my estate and the next, and it promptly melted.

If I listened hard enough, I could hear the sound of the home I'd loved dying around me. I wasn't the only one cursed; all this would be taken to the grave with me. I imagined ice encasing everything once I'd passed. Soon, no one would remember that the castle had existed.

Shivers tracked through Raven's frame, and her teeth chattered. I hated I couldn't do more to warm her than wrap my arms around her, but at least I could offer that.

I held her for a long time. I'd hold her forever if I could.

Two weeks. How could I make sure it was enough?

"We're almost there," I said, stepping back and taking her hand. Her fingers were icy, and I prayed my curse wasn't sinking into her flesh. "I'll light a fire in the front parlor, and that'll warm you up nicely."

Her laugh came out low and husky, and she released my hand to wrap her arm around the back of my waist. "I can think of lots of ways you can warm me, Elion, but we can start with a fire."

I pictured her lying naked on cushions with only the flames lighting the room. I'd part her legs and crawl between them. I'd show her how much she meant to me, how much I ached to claim her.

She was mine, and I was hers, but it wasn't enough to stop my new fate.

With darkness coming, we hurried along the path snaking through the dense woods, holding onto each other to keep from falling on the icy ground.

When we emerged into a small open area overgrown with scraggly grass and stubby trees, we paused at the top of a hill.

"It's beautiful," she said, pointing to my home waiting for us on the taller hill ahead. "I can't wait to see it up close." She leaned into my side. "I can't wait to live there with you."

I pinched my eyes shut for a moment, then opened them and tried to see everything like she did.

I'd admired it, loved it while growing up, but a pall had fallen over it, and there was no wrenching the curse aside. I wanted to see my home gleam with beauty like it had done when I was little one final time.

"Long ago, my ancestors cleared the land on that big hill and built the castle on the top, constructing it with huge slabs of stone they cut on the property," I said. "Back then, they not only owned what remains of the open areas and forests surrounding the castle, but also vast stretches beyond in all directions."

"Did they sell it?"

I smiled down at her, humbled all over again that Raven loved me. My chest ached as the trap tightened.

"They gave land to those who helped them build the castle," I said.

"I like that."

"The castle has stood for thousands of years, and it will do so for at least a thousand more." Long after I was gone and forgotten.

No, I wouldn't be forgotten, not for a while. Raven would remember me.

I took her hand and led her down the hill. We continued through the woods until we reached the base of the rocky hill. The castle stood proudly at the top. When I squinted, I could see how it used to be.

But tattered flags fluttered in the chill wind, and no one called out from the towers to announce our arrival.

Everyone had fled when I was cursed, leaving me to face what was left of my shortened future alone.

We climbed the hill and crossed the drawbridge I'd lowered when I left to travel as a liaison to the human world for the king. If he'd known I'd meet and fall for one of the women—no, that I'd steal Raven from the kingdom—would he have let me play a role in bringing the brides to the fae world?

I stopped at the base of the front steps, and my heart bled. The structure looked sound, but for how long? Cracks zigzagged down the broad steps, and the stone balcony spanning both sides of the large double front doors had broken. Sections jutted up from the frost that even now was sinking deeper into the ground.

The iron knocker had fallen off the right door and lay rusting on the stone. Urns my mother used to fill with flowers had toppled over. Many had broken. Scruffy grass had sprouted through cracks in the walk. When it died, ice coated every surface.

Life tried to find a way, but it failed, just as I would fail.

In a few short weeks, my time in this world would be over.

Raven squeezed my hand. "I still see how lovely it

was in the lines of the building and the gardens surrounding the castle." She cupped my face with her warm hands. "And in you."

"I am scarred. Broken." Only defeat came through in my voice.

"I love your scars. I love you. As for being broken, we all are. But you've gathered the pieces, and you're holding them together."

"For how long?"

"As long as it takes."

If only I had her confidence that everything would turn out right. I'd lost that too.

I kissed her, claiming her mouth as I had her body each night while we traveled.

How long could I keep her here before it was too late to send her away? I didn't want her with me at the end—that would be cruel. That time was rushing closer.

"Let's go inside. I'll warm you." I flashed her a smile, but my heart wasn't in it. I knew what I had to do.

We strode up the broken steps and across the jagged balcony to the front door. The one on the right hung slightly open. I'd closed it when I left, but no lock could keep the fae out. Only respect kept others from breaching another's home.

The door creaked as I pushed it inward, and we stepped into the large foyer.

"This way," I said. We exited through an archway, entering a long hall with doors leading to other parts of the castle. Stairs at either end led to the upper floors.

On the left, I opened a door and ushered her inside

the room where I'd spent much of my time after I was cursed. It was a small room, so it was easier to heat.

I bustled to the fireplace and tindered the wood I'd left here months ago when I traveled to the king's castle.

In no time, flames cast shadows, and warmth flooded the small room.

I took Raven's hand, drawing her away from the sofa I'd sat on so many times. A desk stood in front of one of the three windows where I'd worked, sometimes gazing out at what used to be gorgeous gardens. Remembering what was, and what could never be again.

"I have something to say, and I want you to listen," I said.

She nodded, giving me a soft smile.

I loved her more than anything, and that was why I had to do this.

"I've called for a baishar."

Her delicate brows drew together. "What's a baishar?"

"The silver, winged stallions used to fly through the veil between your world and mine."

Her body twitched, and her voice deepened. "What are you saying, Elion?"

"I want you to leave. Return to your world and live a full life. Find love if you can and . . ." My throat choked off.

How could I say this, do this?

I stiffened my resolve. "When you think of me, smile. I'll feel your warmth wherever I am."

Chapter 43
Raven

"No," I said. "I'm not leaving you, Elion. If you send me away, I'll walk into the sea, calling your name. I'll swim here if I have to."

"Please, Raven." He tried to take my hands. "I haven't much time. My curse . . . Maverna changed it. I only have two weeks left, not a year."

No. It couldn't be. My knees gave way, but he caught and held me. He was going to die, and I didn't know how I could stop it from happening. But leave? I couldn't.

I stepped backward and lifted my chin. "I'm not going." My eyes stung, but I shoved away my tears. "I can't go. Please. Don't do this."

I couldn't bear it. How could he push me away after all we'd gone through to be together? My throat closed off with pain.

"I don't want you to go. Don't you see?" He spoke softly, but I couldn't miss the agony in his voice. The sorrow lining his face. The tortured expression in his eyes. His emotions cut through the anguish expanding within my chest. "I don't have much time left. I can't bear for you to be here when my life ends."

"Two weeks can mean a lifetime. And it doesn't have to be this way. We can stop it. I'll find a way to help you," I said, my heart shattering. I'd do anything, give anything to save him. "I have to be with you, Elion. If I'm not, there's nothing left of me."

"I can't offer you *anything*," he said bitterly. "Look around you, Raven. Everything here is frozen. *I'm* frozen."

No. I wouldn't accept this. I strode up to him and cupped his warm face. "You're not frozen. I feel you, Elion. There's so much warmth in you. So much love. It wraps around me and protects me."

"I'm only warm because you're part of my life," he said gruffly. "You keep the ice at bay."

"I love you. I always will. Please don't ask me to leave. We'll find a way to end the curse. We have to because we're meant to be together. Maverna will never drive a wedge between us. I'll keep you warm and fight to be with you always." My voice broke. "Please. I'm begging. Don't do this. Don't break us."

"Raven," he groaned, conflict creasing his face.

He dropped to his knees in front of me.

My heart pinched so tightly I could barely breathe. I hurled myself into his waiting arms, letting my tears fall freely. "I love you, Elion. So much. Please feel that, know that. It's never going to change."

"I do. Always. I'm sorry I asked you to go." He spoke

into my hair, his warm arms around me. "I never want to cause you pain."

"There is no life for me without you. If you send me away, I'll feel the loss forever." Leaning back in his embrace, I pressed his hand against my chest. "My heart beats only for you."

He placed my hand against his own chest. "And my heart beats only for *you*."

Taking my hands, he kissed them. He urged me to my feet and looked up at me.

"Bae mae frael liethrà, an ular fieair al laitlen ru mae sleedest," he said in a solemn, husky voice. "Bae mae wurth al disulen, al tàirean, als reeg de undelar biswee. Ular tash a-hàis al maen coìlasar. Oi liethràla tash."

The air around us seemed to breathe. I felt as if spring waited for the signal to arrive, to melt everything and restore happiness and life to this castle. But something held it back, something I could *change*. I could make a difference. I could save Elion. I knew this with every fiber of my being.

"The words I spoke bind us together in the fae world and beyond," he said.

"They're beautiful."

"In your language, it means . . ." He sucked in a breath and stared into my eyes. "Be my forever love, the only one to lie by my side. Be with me today, tomorrow, and until the bitter end. Only you can complete me. I love you, Raven."

"I love you. It's perfect."

"Humans call these words a proposal."

"You want to marry me?"

"Always. Forever. Please say you'll be by my side until my dying day."

"I will. I do." My smile broke through my tears.

"I want marriage," he said. "Here, we call it a full matebond, which is a rare thing among the fae. But you are mine, and I am yours. I will always be your humble servant."

"Yes. Yes. Yes." I leaped into his arms and punctuated my words with kisses on his face and neck. "All I want is to be with you. Nothing will hold us back. I'll do everything I can to be with you forever."

He stood, bringing me to my feet with him. A shy smile filled his face, and in his eyes, I read a promise for a future full of love. We just had to grab onto it, hold it close, and never let anyone or anything tear us apart.

A wave of his hand, and jeans and shirt had been replaced with a gown like something out of a fairytale. In a rich ivory and with a smooth bodice, it had a puffy skirt that fell to brush my feet and capped sleeves. My breath caught as I ran my fingers along the smooth fabric.

When I reached up, even my hair had been changed, coiled up on my head in an elaborate arrangement. Teardrop stones hung from my ears, and when I moved my head, they caught the light and sent it shooting around us like stars.

"Elion," I croaked, overcome with love. "This . . . I can't find the words."

"You already have. Seeing the wonder and love on your face makes me feel complete." He pressed his hand against his chest and his old clothing disappeared, replaced with a formal tunic. Bits of silver stitching gleamed in the light, and his hair had been neatly tied at the back of his neck.

A clasp of my hands and a blink, and we stood in front of the altar of a gorgeous, golden chapel. Ice encrusted the room and icicles dripped from the ceiling, but I felt only warmth here. The heat of Elion's love. I'd never be cold as long as he stood beside me.

A smile teased across his mouth, and he bowed. "On Earth, when a couple marries, they speak vows."

I swallowed, and the words blurted from me. "I do."

He chuckled. "I do as well."

"I take you, Elion Daeven Luthaistras Iliric Fendove, to be my lawfully wedded husband," I said, staring up at his dear face. How could anyone call him ugly? When I looked at him, all I saw was love.

"And I take you, Raven Kathryn Wilder, to be my lawfully wedded wife, in this world, the human world, and throughout the realms."

My grin was so big it made my cheeks ache. I stared up at this man I loved more than life itself. "I can't say the words in your language, but may the realms hear it in mine." I closed my eyes and prayed I didn't miss a word. What he'd said to me had been the most beautiful thing I'd ever heard. "Be my forever love, the only one to lie by my side. Be with me today, tomorrow, and until the bitter end. Only you can complete me. I love you."

"Look at your wrist," he said.

I lifted my right hand and my eyes widened. An intricate woven chain entwined around my wrist, but it had been fused into the surface of my skin like a tattoo.

He took my hand, showing me he also had the same mark on his wrist. "We are matebonded forever, Raven. Nothing and no one will tear us apart. Little human, I love you with everything inside me, and that will never change."

He stroked my cheeks with his thumbs and kissed me.

I wrapped my arms around his neck, holding tight. I would never let go. I would never let anything harm him.

This I vowed with everything inside me.

A flash of light made me lean back in his arms. Glitter rained down on us.

Laughing, he lifted me and spun me around, kissing me while the tiny stars floated in the air around us.

I didn't know what would happen next, but I wasn't going to give up. No, I'd fight with everything inside me to be with Elion forever.

Betts and Nuvian were missing, but I hoped to find them here.

Aillun was solidifying his control of the fae throne. He might not realize it, but his rule would be short-lived.

The king was off hunting Maverna, but Follen would catch up to him and bring him to us. After that, we'd find a way to defeat Maverna together.

And Elion, my precious Elion, still had a wretched curse hanging over his head and the clock was ticking. Two weeks!

I'd rip my way through this world and mine to break the curse and save him.

Because we had a love like no other.

Even death would not tear us apart.

~TO BE CONTINUED~

If you'd like to find out what happens next,
look for Ice Lord's Fate, book two and the conclusion
of the Bride of the Fae Series.
Turn the page for Chapter 1...

Ice Lord's Fate

**Elion is mine, and I won't let
anyone steal him away.**

Elion and I have escaped the evil encroaching on the castle and fled to Elion's ice-covered estate. We're finally together, but the peace we find in his childhood home is short-lived. We spend our days working with friends to restore the true king to the throne, something his son and an evil witch refuse to see happen, and our nights clinging to each other.

And the clock is ticking.

Unless I can end Elion's curse, he'll die. In desperation, I search the kingdom, determined to break the witch's curse before it steals him from me forever. I refuse to lose him. He's my life and my love, and I'll lay down my life to save his.

But what if my sacrifice isn't enough?

Ice Lord's Fate is book two in a fantasy romance duology. This series heats to a high sizzle and comes with a guaranteed happily ever after.

Warning: Don't read this book unless you're open to steamy romance, mystery & danger, and you're intrigued by the idea of becoming a bride to a fae ice lord.

Get your copy here.

Series by AVA

Mail-Order Brides of Crakair

Brides of Driegon

Fated Mates of the Ferlaern Warriors

Fated Mates of the Xilan Warriors

Holiday with a Cu'zod Warrior

Galaxy Games

*Alien Warrior Abandoned/
Shattered Galaxies*

Beastly Alien Boss

Bride of the Fae

Ava Ross

Screaming Woods
Orc Me Baby One More Time

Stranded With an Alien
Frost

You can find my books on Amazon.

About the Author

Ava Ross is a *USA Today* Bestselling author of numerous titles. She fell for men with unusual features when she first watched Star Wars, where alien creatures have gone mainstream. She lives in New England with her husband (who is sadly not an alien, though he is still cute in his own way), her kids, and a few assorted pets.

Chapter 1
RAVEN

A scraping sound woke me, and I sat up in bed, my heart thrumming in my ears.

Elion slept beside me; his body relaxed. Something twisted inside me when I caught the expression of pure satisfaction on his face.

I'd put that look there when I gave him the gift of my heart and my body. Nothing would make me happier than to do so every day for the rest of my life.

But what had I heard? I searched the dark room with wide eyes but didn't see anything worth investigating.

Moonlight filtered through the ice-encrusted windows lining the right wall, casting shadows on the furniture placed here and there inside the enormous bedroom. If I let myself, I could be easily overwhelmed by all this. I was living in a freakin' castle!

Seeing the shy excitement on Elion's face after he'd warmed our room made me eager to gush. It wasn't hard. This place, even encrusted with ice, was gorgeous. And his bedroom had to be the nicest suite in the place. My apartment back home could fit inside with room left over for more.

When the scraping sound wasn't repeated, I laid back down, snuggling beneath the blankets while stealing the warmth from Elion he so eagerly gave. He mumbled, and his arms coiled around me, tugging me into his heady embrace.

I wanted so much for us.

Being together was a given.

Breaking his curse was my top priority, of course.

I wanted the chance to see our love grow and deepen.

I clung to the hope that if I loved him enough, I could help him. There had to be a way.

We had less than two weeks to break his curse. The thought crashed through me like a truck going ninety miles an hour hitting a stone wall. My mouth went dry, and tears stung the back of my eyes. I sniffed. It wasn't enough time. That damn witch. She'd changed the rules.

She wanted my Elion dead.

A scratching sound reached me from outside. Was a branch scraping across the siding? Maybe a random creature was racing along the outer sill. Were there squirrels in the fae kingdom?

When the curse was laid on Elion, his world froze solid. Everything had been locked in place at that exact moment, including any potential squirrels.

Elion would create what we needed with magic, just like he had the meal we'd eaten after we'd satisfied our hunger for each other. But everything else would remain locked as it was until the spell was broken.

Koko blinked up at me from where he'd coiled into a fluffy ball at the foot of the bed.

When the scratching sound was repeated, his head snapped around, and he peered toward the window. He bared his little teeth and hissed.

I gulped. Should I wake Elion? He was tired. Using magic to warm our room and bring us food had drained him.

The curse drained him.

Waking him for something as silly as this felt cruel.

It was a stick. A bit of tile dropping off the roof. It was *nothing*.

I flopped onto the bed, but I couldn't get back to sleep.

"All right," I whispered. "Go look at the branch, and *then* you can ignore the sound." I slipped from our bed, shivering when my bare feet touched the floor, and grabbed a wrap from a chair, swirling it around my body to help hold in the heat.

I crossed the room on tiptoe to look out the window.

Something moved across the back lawn, a shadowy being whose feet didn't touch the ground. Long hair flowed out behind her.

I leaned forward, pressing my nose against the glass, trying to figure out who it might be.

Betts? She and Nuvian left the king's castle together to come here. Nuvian wanted to find a way to break the curse and redeem himself in Elion's eyes. Betts . . . crushed on Nuvian, and she'd gone with him.

Elion and I planned to search for them in the morning.

Dense woods, the trees so leaden with ice that the tips of their upper branches nearly touched the ground, marched from the cliffs beyond down to the back lawn.

The ghostly figure bolted toward the woods, the hem of her dark gown fluttering in the wind. A creature unlike anything I'd seen before trotted beside her. A big dog?

My swallow went down hard.

A hyena the size of a pony sniffed the ground before tipping its head back and releasing a stuttered growl. The woman paused, and the beast caught up to her.

I didn't dare breathe. I remained as frozen as this castle, watching through the window.

When she reached the edge of the lawn, she lifted one hand. A path opened in front of her, slicing through the forest. She stepped toward it, but before her feet hit the trail, she turned back.

The woman in the dining room portrait—the one whose eyes seemed to watch me—looked toward Elion's home.

Now I remembered where I'd seen her before. This was the witch, the one who'd changed from a bird into an evil old woman. She'd tried to kill us the day we rode glisteers with the other human women in the forest.

This evil being had cursed Elion.

Her gaze raked up the tall stone building until it

locked on the window where I stood. Hatred flashed red in her eyes.

With a gulp, I flung myself to the side, hiding behind the wall between the windows, shaking like never before. Despite the chill in the air, a bead of sweat hitched down my spine, spreading shivers through me like hoarfrost etching across glass.

Being naked with Elion was the most wonderful thing in the world. Standing in a chilly room while someone watched me? Not so much.

I tossed the blanket aside and tugged my gown over my head, stuffing my feet into my sandals. They were totally impractical footwear, but I was wearing them when we left the king's castle. With quakes tracking down my spine, I wrapped the blanket around my body again, though nothing was going to warm me now.

I didn't have magic. I knew very little about this world I'd married into. But one thing was clear.

The witch who'd cursed the man I loved knew we were together. I bet she knew we'd married.

I counted to ten, then peeked through the glass again.

She still watched.

This time, when she caught my eye, she lifted her bony finger, pointing it at me. A murky yellow mist shot from the tip, blasting against the glass.

A bit of it made its way inside, and it sought me.

Found me.

Engulfed me.

The air around me shimmered.

In a blink, I stood in a mist-filled world made up of

dark clouds and fury. While I couldn't see it, I felt the world churning around me.

I turned, my hands reaching out for anything to grab onto, but finding nothing but air and white mist. Even my feet were planted in a gray-streaked cloud.

Where was I?

Panic roared through me, and I struggled to keep it from grabbing onto me and bolting.

"Elion?" I whimpered. My teeth chattered, and my skin went clammy.

Something shrieked to my left, and I faced that direction with only my stupid human hands lifted to protect me.

Footsteps thundered my way, and a beast unlike anything I'd seen before emerged from the smoke. It was a pony. No, a big dog. A magical mix of a wolf and a saber-toothed tiger.

When it saw me, it shrieked again. It rushed toward me, its long tusks slashing through the air.

Get Ice Lord's Fate!